Escape from Nowhere

She should have been a carefree high school girl but instead Carla was suffering—suffering from want in the midst of plenty.

The plenty was her family's beautiful home and their high standard of living. The want was not a lack of *things*. Carla wanted her father home more, she missed him, and she was sure her mother would stop drinking so much if he were there. She wanted to be able to bring a friend to the house after school, and be sure her mother was "all right." She wanted help from her older sister, Diane, but Diane was away at college, and totally absorbed in her own pursuits.

It was a bad time for Carla—a very bad time to be introduced to the world of marijuana and other drugs. Carla found the way into this world all too easy—the way out was another story. . . .

". . . filled with the world of teenagers, their problems and their often ignored cries for help and understanding."
—*Publishers' Weekly*

ESCAPE FROM NOWHERE

Jeannette Eyerly

A BERKLEY HIGHLAND BOOK
PUBLISHED BY
BERKLEY PUBLISHING CORPORATION

CONTENTS

1

CALL ME CARLA

Call Me Carla.

The best first sentence of the best book I ever read begins that way. The sentence is "Call me Ishmael," and the book is *Moby Dick*. I wouldn't be telling the truth if I said I really understood it. The book, I mean. But Ishmael tells the story of a search. And my story concerns a search, too, but of a different kind.

The main thing to consider about a beginning is not to make it boring. So I'm not going to start by telling when I was born or anything like that; nor when we moved from the west side of Cedar City to the east side so Diane and I could go to the "best" high school and have more "advantages." What a laugh.

I'm not going into how it felt to leave all my old friends behind—kids I'd known since I was in kindergarten—and start in at a strange new school. It was tough. I'll just say that. The only good thing about the move was that I got to have a room of my own. And even having your own room isn't as great as some kids would have you believe. Diane and I have always gotten along very well. She was always very nice to me when I was little and if, after I grew older, she couldn't do much to change or improve me, well, that was my fault not hers. Maybe what I'm trying to say is, that while it was nice to have a room of my own, my father was gone more. Sometimes a month at a time. And last fall after Diane went away to college and there was only my mother and me there in that big house, I wished everything was the way it had been before.

So I guess the real beginning was the day I admitted to myself I had a problem.

The funny thing was, it took me so long to see I had it. Maybe not so funny either. I remember reading in a geography book when I was in about the sixth grade that the Mississippi River starts out as a trickle. And that was the way my problem with my mother started out. So small I didn't recognize it for what it was. It didn't stay that way very long.

I still remember the day, coming out of English class, when Marcie Hamilton asked me if she could borrow a record of Bob Dylan's that I had mentioned that I owned. It isn't a good idea to lend anything that's easily lost or broken, but I liked Marcie Hamilton and would have liked to go around with the same crowd she did. So I said I would bring it to school for her the next day.

Chummily, she hooked her arm through mine. "I've a better idea," she said. "I've got a car. I'll drive you home and pick up the record all in one operation."

In our part of the country you don't tell the person who's offered you a ride home that you'd really rather walk. So I didn't say it. But I would have liked to, though. All the while I was getting my stuff out of my locker and waiting by the door that led to the student parking lot where she said she'd meet me, I was trying to figure out what to do.

I still hadn't thought of a single thing when I saw her bounding down the hall toward me. She had on a fake-fur coat and a hat built like a baby's bonnet with a big band of fake fur around it. She was wearing boots that came up to her knees, and had a pouch-shaped purse that

8

looked like a knitting bag slung on a long cord over her shoulder. If I'd had an outfit like that on, I would have looked ridiculous. But you'll have to believe me when I say that on Marcie Hamilton it looked really very good.

The snow was changing to sleet as we cut across the parking lot. "That's my car over there," Marcie said, waving a fur mitten as big as a catcher's mitt. "The one with the personality."

Outside the car was painted baby blue. Inside, she'd slipcovered everything in sight and for trimming had added yards and yards of blue ball fringe. Between the two bucket seats in front was a container filled with artificial flowers.

"In the summer, I have real flowers growing in there," Marcie said as we settled ourselves in the car. "Geraniums and ivy and things like that. But this is the best I can do in the winter." She fished in her big pouch-purse for a package of cigarettes. "Smoke?" she said, popping one out at me.

I took one, lighting it on the first try, grateful to my sister Diane for teaching me how the summer before. "If you're going to smoke, for heaven's sake, learn how," Diane told me—though I knew she thought it was a stupid habit. "Suck in hard when you light the match—and for heaven's sake, don't hold it as if it were a firecracker about to go off."

Marcie was having trouble with hers. It took three matches, and then when she had the cigarette going, she enveloped herself in such a cloud of smoke that she started coughing. Fanning herself, she inspected the lighted end. "I just may give them up." A few minutes later, when she rolled down the window and tossed it away I threw mine way, too. "The only real benefit from smoking that I can see," she said, "is that a cigarette is a pretty good weapon if some boy you're out with starts to get out of hand."

9

I nodded as if boys getting out of hand, and having to fend them off with lighted cigarettes were my problems, too.

"You'll have to tell me where you live," Marcie said, and when I did she said, "Oh, I didn't know you lived in Parula Park."

She didn't mean to sound surprised, but she did. I guess she thought I didn't look like a girl whose father could afford to live in Cedar City's fanciest subdivision.

I didn't say anything—which was all right. Marcie kept right on chattering away about school and boys until we turned into our drive. The minute she stopped I leaped out of the car, and saying I'd be just a minute, ran toward the house.

The front door was unlocked and as soon as I was inside I stood very still for a second, just listening. There wasn't a sound, except for the faint hum the furnace makes when it's running and the nicking of a naked branch against the living-room window.

I said, "Mother" once, softly; then a little louder. When there was no answer, I could hear my breath which I'd been holding unconsciously, whistling noisily out between my teeth. I sped up the stairs and down the hall to my room. It was the way I'd left it that morning. My pj's were on the floor and the bed was hastily and not-too-well made. My slippers, that Diane declares are a disgrace, peered out from under the desk, looking like two large, unkempt Belgian hares. Even if I'd known for sure that my mother would not be around, my room made me glad that I hadn't let Marcie come in with me.

My phonograph records were in order though. I'm fussy about them—and my books, even if I am sloppy about other things. So it didn't take me long to find the record that Marcie wanted. Actually, I don't suppose more than two or three minutes had elapsed before I was back at the head of the stairs and heard their voices; Marcie's—and my mother's.

I sat down on the top step, holding that phonograph record so tightly against my chest I could have broken it. But though I strained my ears, I couldn't hear what either voice was saying. Step by step, I edged down the stairs until I turned the bend and could see into the living room. My mother was wearing her yellow cut-corduroy robe with the high, fluted collar. Her face was turned away from me but she'd done her hair with care. Sometimes the sight of it—all reddish-gold and glossy, coiled like bright rings of burnished copper with only a stray curling wisp let artfully astray—filled me with a horrible kind of envy because I didn't inherit it, like my sister Diane did. But sitting there in the turn of the stairway, I didn't think about that at all. My only feeling was one of overwhelming, almost crazy relief. My mother was all right. Everything was going to be all right. Even if Marcie Hamilton had managed to get into the house after I thought I had successfully maneuvered to keep her out, *everything was going to be all right.*

I almost tumbled down the rest of the stairs, not stopping until I came to stand beside them, feeling gauche and overgrown like a baby robin—all spots and gaping beak—standing beside its sleek, assured mother.

"How bad of you not to invite Marcella in!" My mother, mock-serious, raised an admonishing finger.

I muttered something and Marcie laughed embarrassedly. "I didn't even knock! I wasn't going to. Rather than have you make another trip clear out to the car, I was just going to wait outside the door until you came out. Then, I was going to ask if you had any of Sonny and Cher's records. But while I was standing there, your mother saw me through the window and opened the door."

11

"I can't stand either Sonny or Cher," I said churlishly, "but here's Bob Dylan."

Marcie took it as if she were receiving the Holy Grail. "I'll take perfect care of it." She took off a shaggy glove and extended her hand to my mother. "I'm *very* glad to have met you." To me, she waved gaily. " 'Bye, Car. See you at school on Monday."

I opened the door for her and watched as she leaped across the dull winter grass and hopped into her car. It was a sad time of day. Although it was only a little after four o'clock, the sky was beginning to gray a little. Lights were already on in some houses up and down the street.

When I went back in, my mother had moved toward the end of the living room and was drawing the draperies. "I *like* Marcie."

"*I* like Marcie." Her tone made me speak defensively.

"Then why didn't you ask her to stay for a little while. Stay for a Coke, or something?"

"I . . . I don't know why I didn't. It didn't occur to me, I guess."

"And leaving her outside in the cold! Honestly, Carla, it really isn't any wonder you don't have friends."

"I thought maybe you were sick . . . that maybe you weren't feeling well." I had not meant to say it, but she'd made me, and right away I was sorry. As she turned to flick on a light, I had seen the look in her eyes. The look a child will give you when he is found in an act of wrongdoing. However, a second later when she faced me it was gone.

"I really wasn't feeling well . . . earlier. In fact, I even thought I might need some of my medicine to pick me up. But then, right after lunch, guess what? Your father called and said he'd be home for the weekend. He hadn't expected to finish in San Francisco until the middle of next

12

week, at least. I said we'd come out to the airport to meet him but he said he was on standby for an earlier flight. If he makes it, he'll be home a little after five. If not, he'll be on the ten-o'clock plane for sure."

As my mother talked she darted around the room, shaking up a pillow, moving an ashtray a trifle closer to a chair in which my father often sat. "You *are* going to change before we go out."

I didn't need to look at myself to know what she meant, still I said, "I didn't know we were going out. Until now, I mean. Are you sure Daddy will want to? Go out, I mean. After being gone from home for so long?"

"Of course, he wants to," my mother said busily. "I've already called The Flame Room for reservations. Now run along. A bath and shampoo—really, Carla, your hair is a fright—will make you look ever so much better. And put on your new dress. I've scarcely seen it on you since we brought it home."

All the while I was getting ready, I kept going over to the window and looking out, watching for the taxi and for my father to get out of it. I remembered the winter I was four and Diane five. The minute it began to get dark we'd run and sit crosslegged in the narrow little front hall of our apartment on Beeler Street waiting for our father to come home.

"Don't start waiting yet," my mother would say. "Daddy won't be home for a long time yet. Better come and play one of your games here in the living room for a while." Sometimes we'd do what she suggested but usually we chose to sit in the hall and play with our dolls until he came bounding up the two flights of stairs to where we lived.

Outside, I heard a car door slam. From my window I could see it was the cab and from it, a moment later, my father's tall figure emerged. He picked up his two bags that the driver had already set out on the ground and walked heavily toward the house.

I hurried downstairs.

Neither my mother or father heard me and I had to clear my throat in a mock-menacing manner and say, "My turn!"

My mother moved to one side of him but she did not take her arm from around his waist. He gave me a hearty hug and a kiss. "You smell good."

"Just soap."

My father grinned. "That's still my favorite flavor for a girl."

"But White Shoulders for a woman?" said my mother, smiling.

"Every time."

He had taken off his coat and muffler and he and my mother were walking arm in arm toward the living room when he stopped. "This is a mistake. Before I even think about having that martini that you say is chilling for me in the refrigerator, I'm going to go upstairs and finish my report."

"Carl! Not the first night you're home!" My mother's voice rose in a wail.

"I'd have finished my work on the plane if a bore with ball-bearing jaws had not sat next to me. But a half hour's work will see it through. I promised Bleymann before I left San Francisco that I'd have it in the mail to him tonight."

"I won't fuss with you!" my mother said gaily. She made little shooing motions with her hands. "You just run along. I'll get my revenge at dinner. I'll order the most expensive entree The Flame Room has to offer. That's where we're going, you know."

My father's study is just an upstairs bedroom we

haven't any use for, but mother has really fixed it up so it isn't bedroomy at all. She has good taste about everything. There are bookcases in the room, a couple of comfortable chairs slipcovered in a tangeriney and off-white print, a coffee-colored carpet and draperies and lots of things on the wall. Mostly these pertain to his business. Plaques, framed awards, group pictures, and several others of my father and J. W. Dowitcher, himself, who is president of the company my father works for.

It was to this study my father went to finish his report, and every time I went up and down the hall from my room to the bathroom, or to Diane's room—she's put all the things she doesn't care if I use in the bottom drawer of her biggest chest—I could see him working.

On about my fourth trip, he called out for me to come in; that he was almost done.

Although I promised not to say a word until he was through, I stood at his shoulder while he worked, watching as he filled in different sections of his report. Although I watched, I wasn't really seeing it. It was too complicated for me to understand. All I really knew about my father's business was that he was doing very well at it and that Mr. J. W. Dowitcher was pleased with him. It seems that not many men who never get to go to college do as well. And no one has ever gone from a Tingle route sales-man—"Tingle Tantalizes Your Taste Buds" is their mot-to—into the main office and from there out into the field to sell the franchise for Tingle to bottling companies in cities all over the United States. No one has, I mean, except my father.

I did not notice when he put down his pen, nor hear him the first time he spoke. Now he swung around in his chair. "I asked if you were giving the boys at school a hard time."

Maybe hearing himself say the words for the second

time made him realize how silly and pointless they were. I mumbled, "Not really," and he looked unhappy. "Sometimes," he said, "it takes a little time. Your new dress is very pretty."

I said, "Thank you," but we both knew it was an empty compliment. The dress was pretty, but not on me. It was too tight across the hips and not tight enough in places it ought to be. I was beginning to wonder why I'd looked forward for three weeks to talking to my father. I was wondering rather desperately what subject we were going to tackle next when my mother appeared in the doorway.

"I'm sorry to interrupt your little *tête-à-tête*, but if you heard the telephone ring it was Pam Newquist. She wondered if by any chance we weren't busy tonight, and if we weren't, if we would go out to dinner with them. A friend of Ken Newquist's has just come in unexpectedly from New York. He . . . the friend . . . is some kind of a what did she call him . . . a security analyst."

"I'd like to go," my father said jovially, "but we happen to be going out to dinner with Carla."

The words were fine and everything would have been all right with me if he hadn't added, "It would be useful to know someone like their friend. Sometime."

That did it. I started for the door. "Oh, for heaven's sake, run along with the Newquists and their friend. I don't mind a bit. Honestly, I don't. The three of us can all go out to dinner tomorrow night, instead."

My mother gave me an impulsive little hug. "I'll go call Pam right away."

My father started to straighten up his desk, then suddenly he stopped. "You're sure you feel all right about this? Absolutely sure?"

"Of course!" I said. "Don't be silly."

Knowing how much they both wanted to go out with

the Newquists I wouldn't have dreamed of answering any other way. But the funny thing was that an hour later when I watched them leave, I still felt the same way.

And that's why I cried. I felt no way at all.

2

FALLING STAR

Something interesting came up for my parents to do on both Saturday and Sunday nights, so the three of us never did go out to dinner. Instead, on Sunday noon we went to a pancake place and on Monday morning when I got up, my father was off on another three-week trip. How's that for an interesting weekend?

At school, nothing happened until Tuesday when I met Marcie as I was coming out of gym. I wouldn't have stopped if she hadn't. "I've been looking for you," she said. "My parents are going out Saturday night and they said I could have some kids over. You can bring a date if you like—I expect most of the girls will. But it isn't necessary," she added hastily, "if you're not going with anyone special."

"I'm not . . . but I'd like to come."

"See you around eight, then, or a little after." She started off, but turned before she'd gone only a step or two. "Say, I've been meaning to ask. Is Diane Devon, the one who graduated from school here last year, your sister?"

I nodded, knowing what was coming before Marcie had said Word One.

"I never would have guessed until I met your mother. They're both so pretty!"

I let my face freeze into the smile I keep especially for

such occasions. "I know. They look amazingly alike."

I'd been on my way to the cafeteria to meet Glenna Eagles for lunch but after I'd met Marcie, I decided to go to the library instead. If I didn't show up, Glenna would go ahead and eat lunch without me. She's a very nice-dispositioned girl and about the only good friend I've made since I started at this school.

That night, I wasn't hungry either and my mother, who usually spends the entire meal nagging at me because I put too much butter on my bread or take two helpings of some starchy food, started picking at me because I wasn't eating enough.

"You have to eat something. If you're not careful, you'll get mononucleosis."

"I wish I would get it," I said, "though it's not likely. It comes from kissing, you know. A girl at school got mono and lost twenty pounds. I should be so lucky."

My mother dabbed at her eyes with her handkerchief. "I don't understand you, Carla. I swear I don't. Sometimes, it just seems to me that you try to be difficult."

"I don't have to try. It just comes naturally."

After that, my mother really did cry. Even when I apologized she went on vaporizing and I finally had to tell her about being invited to Marcie Hamilton's party on Saturday night.

If I'd told her I'd just been selected Homecoming Queen at the State University she wouldn't have been more excited. "Why, that's wonderful! Do you know who else has been invited?"

I said I didn't, but that didn't dampen her enthusiasm. She was just so glad I was going somewhere. She declared it just wasn't "normal" for a young girl to sit at home all the time and read and listen to records, and that Diane certainly hadn't. She reminded me that Diane had not only

20

dated boys from the best families in high school but since she'd been in college she was dating only boys from the best fraternities.

All of which was the truth. But, as I was so often reminded, I wasn't Diane. Still, in the next four days I managed to lose three and a half pounds and by Saturday night when I got ready to go my stomach was a lot flatter and my hips didn't look nearly so fat. Then, because I'd really been so ugly to my mother all week, I let her trim my hair. Since early last summer when I started letting it grow, she's been after me to cut some bangs so I let her do that, too.

"You're just not the type to have so much long stringy hair hanging about," my mother said, as she took one last snip then leaned forward to blow the loose hair from my face.

I looked at myself in the mirror and I did have to admit it looked nice. Well, if not nice, an improvement. The bangs tended to make my eyes, which people tell me are my best (they really mean *only* good) feature, look bigger and darker. And when my mother went and got her own lipstick, I put a little on though usually I don't use any because hardly any other of the kids I know do.

Driving over to Marcie's, I felt happy and a little excited. I was glad my mother had let me take her car. I thought that maybe, at last, there was going to be a sort of turning point in my life. Actually, I didn't want a lot. A nice boy for a friend, somebody who would ask me out now and then to a movie, to play tennis, or go ice-skating; a little crowd of kids to go around with at school.

But no matter how good I felt driving over to Marcie's, by the time I parked the car it had vanished. This party would be no different from all the other parties to which I had occasionally been invited. Nobody would talk to me and if they did I wouldn't be able to think of anything to say. Consequently, I'd just stand around trying to make myself invisible until it was time to go home. That's why I didn't go to mixers any more. Mixers! What a laugh.

I knocked but no one heard me and after standing there for a few minutes, I opened the door and went in. It really was pretty noisy. Upstairs, I could hear young children pounding around, and in the one corner of the living room that was visible to me a boy I didn't know was playing the guitar. A half dozen or so kids were sitting on the floor listening and halfway singing.

I had taken off my coat and put it on top of a pile of other wraps on the window seat when Marcie spied me.

"Oh, there you are! Almost everybody's here, though I expect there will be a few gate-crashers. There usually are. I don't know how the word gets around, but it does." She took my hand and hauled me into the living room as if I were a backward child. "Hey! Everybody know Carla Devon?"

A couple of kids I knew by sight looked up from the couch where they sat and said, "Hi." Gordon Dains and Sandra Baker, both of whom were in my home room, said, "Hi, Car," then went on working on an oversize jigsaw puzzle that was spread out on a card table. And that was the extent of my impact.

A couple practicing a dance step in the middle of the room went right on practicing, the boy with the guitar nodded and the kids listening to him went right on listening.

Marcie having launched me, prepared to leave me. "There are cold drinks in the fridge—everything but beer, my dad doesn't allow it—darts in the basement and Ping-Pong on the porch. That's where I'm going now."

She moved off toward the back of the house and I was on my own. For a while, I stood by the kids who were on the jigsaw and although they were perfectly polite, it was

22

also clear that it wasn't the puzzle they were interested in but each other. The boy with the guitar played a couple of things I asked him to, but he really wasn't very good and one by one the kids who had been listening to him faded away. When he said he had to leave I wandered off again, this time to look for Marcie.

Led by squeals and the small explosive sounds a Ping-Pong ball makes bouncing on a table, I found her. She was playing with Fred Jessup, the kind of a boy I would like to have for a brother, if I had one.

"You can play the winner," Marcie said, lunging across the table to smack the ball out of bounds.

Fred grinned. "She means you can play *me*."

I watched them for a while, but they'd just started a new game before I arrived and the porch was too cold just for sitting. I said I'd come back later.

I was at the door before Marcie called after me. "Hey, do you know Dexter Smith?"

I nodded.

"Well, if he shows up will you come and tell me?"

There was a funny inflection in Marcie's voice and I wondered what the business of Dexter Smith was all about. All evening I had been hearing scraps of conversation that meant nothing to me at all. A whole student life went on that I knew nothing about. I might as well have been going to high school on the moon.

While I'd been on the porch, several more couples had appeared and someone had put on the record player and rolled back the rug. Nearly everyone seemed to be dancing or fooling around in the middle of the floor. The jigsaw table was deserted, though, and I went there. I had picked up a piece and was staring at it, not really seeing it nor looking for the place it was supposed to go, when a voice behind me said, "I bet you don't know what the shape of that puzzle is called."

I turned, not knowing whether the remark had been directed to me or not. But it had been, for there was no one else there except the boy who had made it. A tall, lanky-looking boy behind a pair of the biggest blackest horn-rimmed glasses I've ever seen. His hair was thick and black and curly, and so closely cropped that it looked as if it had been made from the pelt of some small animal.

"Pardon me?"

"That puzzle you're working on. The name of the shape. You know, round."

"A circle?"

"No. Though of course it is circular. But before it was made into a puzzle, it was a painting. By Raphael."

I looked down at the puzzle. Now that I was really looking, I could see that there was a lot of blue in it and already something that looked like a cherub's wing was being built up from among the myriad of many pieces strewn about on the card table. I was really rather astonished. "It doesn't look like Raphael," I said, glad that I knew. "But I don't know what the shape is called."

The boy laughed. "I knew you wouldn't. It's called a tondo." Suddenly he was serious as he had been gay a moment before and he looked at me almost anxiously. "Do you think this conversation is . . . dumb?"

I shook my head, but he still seemed worried. "No . . . I like it."

"You're not just saying that?"

"Sometimes when I go to the library I look at art books. Those big, beautiful ones they won't let you take out for fear something would happen to them. I . . . I like art. I take it at school. Next to English it's my favorite subject." The words had burst out of me without thinking what I was going to say. I smiled a little self-consciously and the boy was smiling, too.

"Usually, when I try to make conversation with a girl,

you know—when I say something like I said to you, she just looks at me as if I were some kind of a nut. I don't seem to have the gift for ordinary conversation."

"I don't have it either." But instead of being embarrassed to confess it, the lack now seemed funny. "Would you believe it, but sometimes when I'm with a boy the only thing I can think to talk about is the book I'm reading." I couldn't help laughing. "When I mention the word 'book,' they just fade away. You know, like the cat in *Alice in Wonderland.*" I fitted a piece of the puzzle into the place and my happiness gave way to a new feeling. "I'd think . . . Marcie would be easy to talk to."

"Marcie?"

"Marcie Hamilton," I said patiently. "She lives here. She's the girl who's giving the party." In spite of his talk about Raphael and tondos I was beginning to think that maybe he was some kind of nut after all.

The boy grinned. "Don't know her. I'm a friend of her brother, Dave. He said if he wasn't back from the library when I got here, to come in and wait. I didn't know there'd be a party going on. I felt pretty much out of it until I started talking to you." He nodded toward the sunroom which lay behind us. "Do you suppose we could go in there and sit down? It would be a better place to talk."

The room was in semidarkness and I had to peer to see if the couple I'd seen necking in there a little while before had left. "Maybe for a little while."

There was a big, squishy old sofa out there and we sat on that, looking out into the living room where the kids were still dancing and fooling around. Marcie and Fred had finished their game and were doing some kind of trick with a full glass of water held to the ceiling with a broomstick. It was a little like sitting in a darkened theater and watching a play take place on the stage before you.

It was an absolutely painless way to get acquainted.

Watching and talking, I mean. His name was Tom Willard, he was nineteen, and he'd graduated from George Washington High on the other side of town. That's where I'd gone my sophomore year and where I'd still be going if we hadn't moved.

Right after graduation, Tom's family had moved out of town—his father was transferred—but he'd stayed on in Cedar City because he was earning really big money on a road-building gang. Now he was driving a delivery truck, and pumping gas at a filling station. When spring came and road-building started again, he'd go back to that. By the following fall, he figured he'd have enough money to take him through his first year at the university.

All of this didn't come out all in one piece the way I'm telling it but easily and naturally, without a single trace of feeling sorry for himself because he had to put himself through college.

"At least, the Army's not going to get me so I'll be able to finish once I'm really started. I tried to enlist right after I graduated but they turned me down. They seem to have some quaint idea that their soldiers ought to be able to see better than I do." He took off his glasses to polish them and even in the dimness I could see how nearsighted he was. My sister, Diane, has eyes like that—so large and blue with such great dark pupils you could drown yourself in them. Except she wears contacts instead of glasses now and you can really see how pretty her eyes are.

He'd just put his glasses back on when the front door opened and a boy came in. I'd never met Marcie's brother, Dave, but I knew without asking that it was he. He had the same V-shaped face that Marcie has and the same color hair—the shade my mother calls auburn and that kids call red, which of course isn't really red at all.

Tom got up. "If we're going to go I expect we'd better

get started. The meteor shower tonight is supposed to be a good one. That's how Dave and I got acquainted—at the observatory. We were both out there one night a month or so ago when there was something particularly interesting going on." He signaled to Dave who had started moving toward us, then turned to me. "I don't want to take you away from the party, but if you'd like a ride home I'm sure Dave wouldn't mind going along."

For one wild moment I thought of accepting, then coming back later and picking up my mother's car.

"Thanks for asking, but I drove over myself."

"Another time. And look up 'tondo' when you get to a dictionary. I never did get the opportunity to display my erudition on the subject." He grinned. "I see Dave has been waylaid by a female. I'd better go and rescue him."

Dave rescued himself, however, before Tom could reach him and a minute later both boys were out the door.

For me, the party was over, too. I found my coat, then I went to look for Marcie to say good-bye. I found her in the kitchen pouring a chili-like mixture from a big kettle into an ironstone tureen.

"Don't go now!" she cried. "Just when we're getting ready to have this divine food!"

It really did look delicious, but I shook my head. "Better if I don't stay. I'm dieting."

"I noticed. You really aren't so . . . you really are thinner."

I decided to take it as a compliment. "I don't have to go this very minute, if there's something I can do to help . . ."

"If you hold the kitchen door for me, I'll bring in the tureen—it weighs a ton. Everything else, I think, is on the table."

At the sight of the food everyone surged into the dining room giving me the opportunity to slip back into the kitchen and down a hall that led to the front of the house. I had my hand on the knob when the door seemed to open by itself.

I'd told Marcie that I knew Dexter Smith. And I did—in a way. Some kids in high school it's impossible *not* to know. Not always because they're so important but just because they're themselves.

Dexter was both. He'd been editor of the annual his junior year. And he was smart. In the top ten percent of our graduating class at the last reckoning. Not that that's so great. I was, too, and it hadn't got me anyplace at all.

But standing there in Marcie's front hall I was too startled by Dexter Smith's proximity to be reviewing his past accomplishments. And he, I think, was almost as astonished to find himself face to face with a strange girl. For face to face is what we were. A circumstance contributed to by the fact that Dexter is not a tall boy and I am tall—for a girl.

"And whose big baby are you?" His smile was easy, his tone faintly mocking.

I blushed and stammered. "I am . . . I was just leaving."

"So it seems." Still smiling, he looked away from me and over my shoulder. "Party over?"

"No. They're just getting ready to eat. If . . . if you'll excuse me I'll tell Marcie . . ."

But there was no need. For Marcie, herself, had suddenly appeared. "Dexter," she said, "I *told* you." She really looked quite nervous. "My parents aren't home and I just . . . well, I just don't dare."

"But I'm straight, Marcie. Scout's honor. Look." He took off his heavy jacket and stepped from the shadowed front hall into the doorway of the brightly lighted living room. He smiled faintly, held two fingers to his forehead in salute. Though he wore his blond hair longer than I

28

really like on a boy, he looked nice. Scrubbed and neat, wearing a pullover sweater of the shade of blue I like best.

"And you haven't got Lisl . . . or anybody . . . out there in the car?"

"Scout's honor," Dexter said again.

"Well . . ." Although Marcie's tone was still doubtful and she did not look happy, I knew she was weakening and that in another minute Dex would have joined the party.

Neither of them noticed me as I left, and I did not spend much time trying to figure out what the interchange between them had been all about. For as I stepped out into the cold clear night a falling star streaked across the heavens. It seemed the best of omens, maybe because I knew that Tom Willard had seen it, too.

3

BLOWUP

Right from the first, I told myself that Tom Willard wouldn't call me.

But it was reverse thinking—in my heart I thought he would.

Maybe you do that, too. Tell yourself an untruth as a protection. I've been doing that almost as long as I can remember; telling myself I'd get a "C" or worse on an exam so that the "B plus" or "A" I nearly always received would be sweeter.

By the time a week had passed, however, the game was no longer worth playing. For Tom didn't call. My only consolation was that I'd had the good sense not to mention him to my mother. After several days of unsuccessful probing—who had been at the party, had I met anyone "interesting," what kind of house did the Hamiltons have, was it "nicer" than ours, and so on and so on and so on—she had finally given up. Actually, I did tell her everything I could think of, except that part about Tom and me. My mother and I have little enough to talk about as it is.

I buried myself once again in the old familiar routine of school and homework. But even that was not too bad. I've always liked going to school—tell most kids that and they look at you as if you needed to have your head examined—but I really do. And even homework isn't too bad unless you have a sadistic teacher.

The person it was hardest not to tell about Tom was Glenna Eagles. Though she didn't date herself, she would have been glad—really glad—to hear that I'd met a nice boy and that I might be going out with him. But something kept me from telling even her. Each day after school I hurried home so I could be near the telephone. Once I passed up going to a movie with my mother for the same reason. And another time Glenna Eagles asked me over to her house in the evening to study—we both were in advanced track in math and it really helped to put our brains together—but I was afraid to go for fear I'd miss Tom's call.

It was on a Friday and almost two weeks had elapsed since Marcie's party and my meeting with Tom, when Glenna asked me again. We were coming out of history last class period when she said, "We're having pasties for dinner. I won't tell you what they are—you really have to see them to appreciate them. Anyway, my mother said I could ask you over. After dinner we can study." As we headed toward our lockers which are in the same corridor, she added, "Maybe you could come home with me right now. It would be simpler all the way around. I'll go down to the office with you and you can call your mother and see if it's all right."

"Oh, I'll call her," I said. I didn't want to sound rude right after receiving an invitation, but neither did I want anyone listening to the conversation I would have with my mother over the telephone. My intuition about things like this is very good. I can't explain it, but sometimes I can *feel* what is going to happen. Even before my mother said "hello," I knew she was having one of her bad days. Sometimes when some of her friends are there, notably Lil Forrester whom I simply cannot stand, or if she'd been downtown shopping, she sounds very gay.

It was noisy in the office—it always is right after school is out—and I leaned close to the receiver, cupping my hand around my mouth as I told my mother what I wanted to do.

"Then you won't be home to dinner." She said this in a particularly flat and expressionless voice and of all the various tones that she uses for certain occasions, this is the one that irritates me most. Answering her I tried to conceal it, but I'm afraid I wasn't too successful.

"If I go over to Glenna's house for dinner," I said, "I'm afraid I can't be home for dinner, too." I laughed to take the sting out of my words, then to make it worse again I said, "But of course I won't go at all, if you really mind."

"Mind? Why should I mind?" My mother's laugh was even more artificial than mine.

"All right," I said, "I'll be home in just a little bit."

"No, Carla, I *want* you to go. Don't hang up. Carla, are you still there?"

I smiled, then answered. "I'm here, Mother."

"You run along with your little friend and have a nice time. I'll be all right. I don't mind at all, really. I . . . I don't know what's wrong with me. I guess I was just feeling a little headachey when you called. But I'm fine now. Just fine."

"If you're positive," I said.

"Positive."

"Well, then, I'll see you later. Glenna will drive me home."

I hung up the receiver, looked at the moist palm of the hand that had held it. I could feel a small trickle of perspiration running from wrist to elbow, but worse was the feeling inside me. Every word my mother had said, everything *I'd* said had sounded as if we were both reading from a prepared script. Instead, we were each playing a part in a real-life play.

I went to find Glenna and tell her my mother had said yes.

I always like going to the Eagles. There are such a lot of them and they are all so gay it seems like more. They don't have much money—but you somehow never think about that while you're there.

It's even more interesting to set the table when everybody's glass is different and no two plates are the same. That's because Mrs. Eagles gets all of their dishes, and lots of their clothes, too, at the Salvation Army store.

The rest of their house is full of surprises, too. Like the old player piano in the dining room and about a thousand rolls of music that they keep in an old tin pie-cupboard beside it. Mr. Eagles got the whole works for ten dollars at an auction. They've a regular piano in the living room that's in good tune, a cello tied together with a piece of rope, a phonograph and recordings of every symphony and opera I'd ever heard of, and books . . . I can't tell you how many books. They were everywhere. There was even a little bookcase in the bathroom. And in the kitchen there was always a book—rather spotted and blistered from water—propped above the window in the sink where Mrs. Eagles washed the dishes.

Mrs. Eagles beamed when she saw us. She is a soft, comfortable-looking woman with almost white hair and pink cheeks. She kissed Glenna, leaving flour on her cheek, then me. "You're just in time! I've cut up the meat and have the suet all ready for the crust. I'll put it together while you two chop the potatoes and the onions."

The pasties were fun to make. On each circle of crust went a big spoonful of potatoes, one of onions, another of meat and a sprinkle of salt and pepper. Then the crust was folded up and over, sealed up tight and they were ready for the oven.

They smelled so delicious baking I could hardly stand it and later when we all gathered around the big dining-room table and ate them, it was heaven. Mr. Eagles said that even a cold pastie was not to be scorned. His father had been a coal miner in West Virginia and his mother made pasties for him to take down into the mine for his lunch. Finding out that his father had been a miner helped me understand Mr. Eagles better, too. Glenna had once told me that he didn't finish high school until after he was married, but now both he and Mrs. Eagles took turns going to night classes at the university and that Mr. Eagles was working toward a degree.

When the last pastie had been devoured—Mr. Eagles noting regretfully that there wouldn't be one for *his* lunch the next day—Glenna and I did the dishes and then got to our studying. We finished a little before ten and then just talked until about ten thirty when Glenna drove me home. She waited in the drive until I had the front door open and blinked the porch light to show I was safely inside.

At that very instant my happiness evaporated.

I've seen the ads that say vodka hasn't any smell, but that isn't true. I could smell it the minute I stepped inside. Lights were on all over the house. Even in the kitchen the tube light was on over the sink and the overhead light blazed away as well. On the counter was an empty vodka bottle, an empty ice-cube tray and an uncooked, thawing TV dinner.

I shut my eyes and put my hot face up against the refrigerator door. Guilt lay like a weight in the pit of my stomach. I should have known this would happen. I rinsed out the glasses and put them in the dishwasher. I put the ruined TV dinner and the empty vodka bottle in a garbage sack and carried it outside. Then I went upstairs.

The door to my mother's room was shut and no sliver of light shone beneath it. I stood there for a moment then continued to my room. If the hall had not been carpeted, if the whole house had not been so still, I do not think I would have heard the steady, bleating sound the telephone receiver makes when it has not been replaced. Certainly, sitting there in the shadowed recess by the window seat I would not have noticed the phone at all.

Almost unthinkingly, I picked up the receiver, cradled it, and went on when I was seized by a sudden and almost paralyzing fear. *Perhaps it was no accident that the receiver was off the hook.* Perhaps . . . I could not let myself envision it. I tried to run but it was like fleeing pursuing peril in a nightmare.

I flung open the door to my mother's room. Half-expecting to find it locked, the impact propelled me stumbling into the darkness. I fumbled for the light switch by the door and in my terror could not find it. I ran toward the bed, feeling for my mother's face. As if from far away, I could hear my own voice babbling, "Mama, Mama, Mama," screaming "Wake up, Mother! Wake up! Wake up!"

When she turned, raised herself on her right arm my panic gave way not to relief but to fury. Scrambling from the bed, on the first wild try I found the switch on the bedside lamp and glared down at her. Although her clothes were disheveled, she was still fully dressed and the bed had not been turned back. "Don't look at me like that," she whimpered. "I . . . I was waiting up for you . . . to tell you . . . good news, but I got so sleepy . . . so awf'lly, awf'lly sleepy . . ." She paused, and a shy, foolish smile touched her lips. ". . . I just took a li'l nap until you got home . . ."

"I thought you were dead!" I knew I was screaming, but I didn't care. "When I saw that you'd taken the receiver off the hook, I thought you . . . you'd . . ."

"The re-ceiv-er . . ." My mother said it as one might a

foreign word whose meaning was slowly becoming clear. "Oh, my God! The receiver . . . the phone . . ." She half fell as she got to her feet, steadied herself on the footboard of the bed and started unevenly toward the door. Then she stopped. "It . . . it was a boy, Carla . . . a boy with a nice voice . . . for you. . . ."

Her face was stricken but it did not move me. I stood, as if carved of ice waiting for her to go on. "And then . . . ?"

"And then . . . I don't remember."

"Did he tell you his name? Leave a message? Anything?"

Again, the fatuous smile. "I forget. I don't know why. I . . . I just forget what he said . . ."

"I know why you forgot," I said. Something inside me seemed to snap. "You forgot because you were drunk. You were so drunk you forgot to put the phone back on the hook. You were so drunk you forgot to do anything except fall into bed."

"Carla, wait! It wasn't like that . . . I . . . I can explain. I wasn't feeling well . . . a headache . . . you know, the doctor said . . . where are you going, Carla! Don't go, baby, don't go!" Her hands were pulling at me and at the sleeve of my sweater. She had started to cry, but all feeling seemed to have left me. With her still stumbling along behind me, still clutching, I walked down the stairs, opened the front door, and went out into the night.

I did not feel cold, and my mother's cries coming from the still-opened front door where she stood, sounded tiny and unreal. I did not think she would follow me—she does not like to be out at night alone. But still I ran. Since then, I have read that fear itself does not cause running, but that the running itself is the cause of fear.

I cannot prove it. But as I ran, faster and faster, terror of a different kind overtook me. I no longer knew from what I was running. My mother . . . a situation I was powerless to handle . . . or myself? It didn't seem to matter. My feet pounded on the sidewalk, mismatched the pounding of my heart. Even after the light turned from green to red, momentum carried me forward. I heard the screech of the car's brakes as I fell, heard a car door slam.

"Man," a boy's voice said, "was that ever a narrow one. Are you hurt—much?"

I shook my head. "Just my knee . . . a little." Already, I'd clambered up over the curb and was trying to stand.

"Easy," he warned. "Easy does it. Here, I'll help you hop over to the car and I'll drive you home. You must live around here, or you wouldn't be running around at night crossing streets on red lights, without a coat on."

"I . . . I'm all right." Except for my right knee which was smarting, and for shivering so I could hardly talk, I did seem to be. "I . . . I'll just walk . . . where I'm going." At this point, going home seemed preferable to going off into the night with a strange boy. But when I was standing straight again and looked at his face, I saw that he was not strange at all.

Recognition struck him, too, at the same moment.

"Well, I'll be . . ." He grinned, snapped his fingers. "I know you. Weren't you at Marcie Hamilton's the other night?"

I nodded.

He said, "I'm Dexter Smith," and I said, "Yes, I know."

4

JASON

"You needn't answer if you don't want to," Dexter said, "but were you going someplace when I almost smashed into you—or running away from something?"

Dexter had put his coat around my shoulders and the car was warm but I was still shivering. "R . . . running away . . . from something."

"From home, no doubt." He cast a quick glance in my direction to see if he was right, but when I looked away he laughed. "Listen, baby, you don't have to pretend with me. I know all about it. Of all the things that happen to be wrong with the world, you can put home and parents right at the top of the list. If you've just found it out, welcome to the club."

A stoplight loomed ahead of us and as Dexter brought the car to a stop, he turned to grin at me. "One thing's for sure. You'll not be wanting to go home. At least, for a while."

"I don't care if I never go home." I had let the words burst out of me without thinking, and although I knew they were childish I didn't care.

"That's the old fight," Dexter said. "And that being the case, the evening can continue according to plan."

Not once since I'd got in the car had I really watched where we were going. The neighborhood through which we were now traveling was one that I had never seen before. Not good, not bad, but one that was in the sad process of being in between. Mr. Reddy, my social studies teacher, only a few weeks before had been explaining how neighborhoods decay and this, I thought detachedly, was it. Rooming houses, big old homes with rickety outside staircases that had been converted into apartments, small shops, beer parlors, pizza places, and too many neon signs.

It could, I supposed, have been like any of a dozen other places in Cedar City—and I expect in your city, too.

When, just a little later, Dexter stopped the car I was surprised. He got out, came around to my side. "If your knee hurts you can lean on me."

I shook my head. Not only was Dexter no taller than I, he was also slight. If I really did lean on him, I was afraid he might fall down.

There was an "Apartment for Rent" sign in the front yard of the building before which we paused. At one time, certainly, it had been nice. Built of brick and stone, two entrance lights as big as honeydew melons guarded its entrance. Only one was lighted, but above the doorway I could see the words "The Lotus" carved into the stone.

Dexter opened the door, held it for me. The vestibule was small, stuffy, and so hot you could smell it. Unclaimed magazines and newspapers lay in an untidy heap on the floor. An old steam radiator, the kind I remembered from the house on Beeler Street where we'd lived when I was very small, hissed and sizzled beneath a brass-framed bank of name plates on the wall above it.

Pushing a button next to a name near the top of the list, he spoke into the tarnished mouthpiece. "Dex," he said. "And friend." He turned unsmilingly, looked at me as if he might be seeing me for the first time, then said into the phone, "She's straight, but she's O.K!" Then he raised his voice and I thought for a moment he was going to be angry. "You can count on it. And me."

The door made an unpleasant buzzing sound and Dexter grabbed it just in time, shoving me into a mustard-colored hallway. In the dim light, his face looked pasty. "You heard what I said—out there?"

I nodded.

Dexter grinned. "Well, it's not quite as cops and robbers as it sounds. But this apartment belongs to a friend of mine—an older fellow. He doesn't mind if I and some other kids he knows drop in now and then and make themselves at home even when he's not there. Actually, I've got a key of my own, but usually I phone up first to see if anybody's there."

He took my arm. "My friend's apartment is on the third floor. Do you think you can make it all right?"

Again, I nodded. Not only had my knee stopped hurting but I felt as if I were walking in a dream. If I weren't dreaming, what was I doing there?

We started to climb, pausing on each floor, until we reached the top. There a cluster of orangish bulbs mounted in a wall bracket cast a faint glow down the longish hall which lay before us. Again Dexter took my arm, hurrying me along past a dozen or more closed doors. Behind several of them I could hear scraps of music coming from a television set or radio. Behind one, I heard a woman crying and a man's voice raised in anger.

When Dexter stopped, I stopped, too, peering around his shoulder at a printed business card thumbtacked to the door before which we stood. "JASON DE PLEINE," I read, "Dealer in Rare Books, Curios, *Objets d'Art* —By Appointment Only." This was followed by a business address and telephone number that, in the dim light, was in too small type for me to read.

Dexter knocked lightly, a series of little taps, some long, some short. Almost at once, there was the sound of a lock being turned and a second later the door opened.

In a second, we were both inside. The hall in which we stood was so dimly lighted that if Dexter had not said, "Hi, Lisl," I wouldn't have known whether the person who had admitted us was a boy or girl. Then I saw that although she was wearing skinny, boy-type pants and had a sort of short tentlike poncho pulled over her head she was indeed a girl, and a very pretty one at that.

"Lisl," Dexter said, "this is . . ." he paused, snapped his fingers.

"Carla Devon." Although I supplied my name as quickly as I could, it was not quite quick enough, for the girl, Lisl, was laughing, I thought, quite hysterically. "Oh, come now, Dexter! You told me she was O.K., and you don't even know her name!" She reached for my hand. "It's all right, honey. Any friend of Dexter's is a friend of mine." She laughed again, leaning limply against the door through which we'd just entered.

"You're stoned, baby," Dex said. His tone was fond. The one a parent might use in talking to a naughty but still lovable child. "You're stoned, and I've not even started to fly. But business before pleasure. And I'd promised Jason I'd make a drop . . . drop something off for him. And pick a little something up." As he talked, he took his coat from my shoulders and removed a small package from one of its pockets.

Lisl reached for it. "Is that for me?"

Dex grinned but he did not release the package. "You don't need it. It's for me. And my friend. If she's interested." Propelling Lisl before him, he moved from the hallway to the living room where he deposited her in a chair. She sat quite still, looking, as nearly as I could tell, at the changing patter of colored lights that flickered around the room. Actually, there wasn't much else to see—though what there was, was queer. A continuous string of blue Christmas-tree lights outlined the moulding around the ceiling. A daybed, covered with a paisley throw; a coffee table spilling newspapers and magazines onto a rumpled shag rug. An ash tray was overflowing. If there were any curios, rare books, or objects of art they were being kept somewhere else.

There were only a few chairs in the room, but cushions and pillows were strewn everywhere. On the floor there was a mattress covered with a quilt, and on it two boys and a girl sat crosslegged, smoking. They moved further apart when they saw us, and one of the boys reached behind him for two more cushions which he tossed in our direction when we sat down. A little exchange of greetings followed. The two boys, neither of whom I'd seen before, were called Chip and Stomper, but the girl turned out to be Daisey Benson who had been in my home room in junior high.

Despite the queer lights and the apartment's furnishings—or lack of them—the kids themselves were so relaxed and friendly that when Dex offered me a lighted cigarette I took it without thinking. Yet the minute I had it in my hand. I knew there was something different about it. Not smooth and firm like a regular cigarette, but smaller and thinner, too. I could see its tip glowing in the dimness. It seemed to be burning up before my eyes when Dex prompted me. "Take a drag. It won't hurt you."

The boy called Chip leaned forward into the circle, speaking earnestly. "That's the good thing about grass. The best thing. It won't hurt you and you can't get hung up on it. It'll make you happy, baby. Happy." He laughed softly. "Just don't waste it. If you don't want a drag, pass it on."

"Next time." As I spoke, I awkwardly offered the

cigarette to Stomper who sat next to me. In the small space of time I had held it, the cigarette seemed to have reduced itself almost by half.

Stomper took it, and enveloping it in cupped hands, inhaled deeply. There was a happy murmur around the circle. The cigarette passed on. Daisey, Chip and Dex taking it in turn. Before I had time even to think, Dexter was again leaning toward me. Sleepily, he exhaled a cloud of heavy, sweet-smelling smoke in my direction, his outstretched hand holding the cigarette.

I could feel the heat from its glowing ash as I took it from him.

"Go on." Dex's voice was soft, approving.

Remembered fragments of things I'd read flashed through my mind. "Grass" was marijuana—the boy called Chip had said that. And marijuana was also called "pot" and this was a "pot party"! I felt like laughing. What a monstrous joke it was! What wasn't funny was Dexter's kindness to me. Without any questions he had accepted me. He had introduced me to his friends and they had warmly welcomed me. It would not only be rude to refuse, but surely there could be nothing wrong in taking a single puff of the cigarette. And it wouldn't hurt me.

I put the soft moist end of the cigarette between my lips and inhaled—not so deeply that I would cough or choke—but enough to feel the acrid burning in my mouth and throat. Already, Stomper was holding out his hand to take what remained of the cigarette from me and Dexter was whispering, "Good girl. The next time around will be easier, and the time after that easier still, until . . ." His face was very close to mine, so close that the size of his eyes seemed magnified. ". . . until things don't seem so lousy any more and you can begin to believe . . . believe in people again."

I watched curiously as Stomper took a straight pin from

his lapel. He inserted it through the end of his cigarette, which now was almost too short to hold, inhaled deeply and passed it on. I did not see who finally ground it out or lighted a new one, but when it came to me I took a single puff as I had done before.

Nothing had happened to me that first time around—no doubt, I thought, the smoke had to go squishing around down in one's lungs before any of the wonderful things that Dexter, or the boy named Chip, said would happen. For the time being, though, it was quite enough for me to be in this pleasant company, to have all the ugliness of the early part of the evening erased and forgotten.

At some point, someone—I think it was Daisey—left the circle to put a stack of records on the phonograph. The music was haunting, melancholy, and the instrument being played was a sitar, which I had never seen but had heard of.

There was a murmur of approval from the circle and after a little silence someone started talking about Indian philosophy and the value of meditation. The necessity for it. Everyone added something, even Lisl—whom I'd almost forgotten about—who presently drifted over to join us. I should say, that everyone added something to the conversation except me. It was all over my head and if anyone had asked my opinion I would not have known what to say.

It was all so interesting that, a little later when Daisey said it was midnight, I couldn't believe it. Daisey laughed. "My mother didn't exactly believe me when I told her I was going to the library tonight to study." She got up from the mattress, stretched and yawned. "And now she's going to believe me even less. But that's her problem, not mine. Anybody want a ride?"

"I'm staying a while longer," Chip said.

Stomper and Lisl said, "Me, too."

"I'll take Carla home and come back," Dexter said. He held out his hand to me as I clambered to my feet.

There were some scattered "good-nights" as we found our way through the dimness back to the front hall where we'd left Dex's pea jacket. This time when he tried to make me put it on, I refused. "I'm not cold now."

"Silly girl. It's winter. You'll be cold as soon as we go out."

I shook my head. "You can put your arm around me." I'd never in my life said anything like that to a boy before, but the words had emerged so lightly and naturally they didn't seem brazen at all.

"Well, wear the coat until we get to your house, at least," Dexter said. "This sweater I'm wearing will be plenty warm enough for me."

I'd forgotten all about my knee and outside on the sidewalk we laughed as we ran, side by side, to the car. It even seemed funny when Dex couldn't find the ignition key and funnier still when it turned up in the pocket of the pea jacket where he, himself, had put it.

Dexter turned on the radio but after trying all the stations and not finding anything he liked, he snapped it off. "I've better music inside my head than that." We both laughed, then drove on, perhaps two or three blocks in silence, before Dexter added what appeared to be an extension of his sentence. "You can't hear it. You didn't smoke enough. But even if you had, you wouldn't hear my music. See what I see. Know what I know. But you'd have your *own*. That's what makes the scene so great. It's hard to explain. It's best just to have it happen."

A stoplight loomed ahead and as Dex brought the car to a stop, a police car pulled along beside us. Not until then had I noticed that the intersection was still twenty or more feet ahead of us. My stomach gave a funny lurch.

The driver of the police car was rolling down the car window on his side and motioned me to do the same to mine. Leaning out, he yelled across me to Dexter, "I don't much like the way you're driving, buddy. Pull up there to the traffic signal where you belong, or I'll give you a ticket."

Dexter swore under his breath, but to the officer his words were polite and his tone meek. "I'm sorry, sir. I'll be more careful in the future."

The stern visage peering in at us cracked into a smile. "O.K. Get along home. Both of you."

The police car moved on, turned the corner, and was gone. In the meantime, Dex had pulled up to the intersection and the light had changed from red to green to red again. In the diffused light from the dashboard his face looked pasty. "I was afraid there for a minute that the fuzz had me cold. A narc wouldn't have been fooled for a minute."

"Fuzz?" I repeated. "Narc?"

Dexter laughed, but there was no amusement in it. "You *are* an innocent. I'll explain to you sometime. If you'd like to know."

"I'd like to know. But now, I think you'd better take me home." Although the car was warm and I was still wearing Dexter's coat I had started shivering again. The neighborhood, however, was one that I recognized and when I told Dexter where I lived he knew exactly how to get there. In less than five minutes we were turning into Parula Park. I pointed down the block.

"Ours is the white house. The one with the breezeway where . . . where all the lights are on."

When Dexter grinned he looked like a satyr. "A warm welcome for the wanderer on a cold night."

"You needn't go up to the house with me," I said, when Dexter stopped the car. "I . . . I'm not afraid."

"Whatever you say. I would, if you thought it would do any good. But sometimes an outsider can make a sticky situation even stickier."

"My mother really can't say too much," I said. "Or, at least, she had better not." It was big talk—and none of it was true. All the pleasant memories of my evening with Dexter were now replaced by the anger and misery that had filled me when I'd gone running out of my house into the night almost three hours before. It was all there waiting for me.

I shrugged out of Dexter's warm coat and had my hand on the door when he stopped me. "If you won't wear my coat, at least take my sweater. You can give it to me at school sometime. I won't be needing it." He shucked the sweater, a pullover, as he spoke, his voice muffled as his head disappeared inside. His hand brushed mine as he emerged. "Put it on. No arguing." He was very serious. "United we stand. Divided we fall. Right?"

"R . . . right." I felt I might cry. "Thank you . . . for looking after me."

"Any time." He leaned across me, opened the door. His face was very close. "Call me at my grandmother's if you need anything. Mrs. Jasper Smith in the phone book. If I'm not there, leave word. She's a lot more interested in the Seminole Indians than she is in me. Even so, she's sweet and likes to be cooperative."

The minute I was out of the car I started running. I looked back, saw Dexter waiting and was glad.

The front door was unlocked as I was certain it would be. No matter what I had done, I couldn't imagine my mother locking me out. Still, I was relieved. I snapped off the porch light as a signal to Dexter, then watched from the window as his car disappeared down the street.

When I turned around, my mother was coming down from upstairs. She was wearing the gold corduroy robe but it was rumpled and untidy and her face was ravaged with tears. She wasn't drunk any more.

"I . . . I thought I heard you."

"Yes," I said, unnecessarily, "I'm home."

As my mother came toward me—slowly, cautiously, as if she was afraid I might go running out into the night again—I could feel tears on my cheeks. She looked terrible. So, of course, did I with my bloody knee, one stocking held together only by a web of threads and a great ragged tear in my best wool skirt.

"I'm sorry, Carla," my mother said. She sank down on the stairs and began to cry soundlessly.

"Don't! Mother, please!" I cried. "I shouldn't have done what *I* did, I'm sorry. Please don't cry. Please!" I was like a child begging forgiveness, yet only a little while ago I had hated her. I did not understand myself.

My mother raised her face. "I didn't know where you were. I thought you might not come back." Then she began to cry again.

"But I did come back!" I cried. "I fell down and skinned my knee a little, but that's all. We'll go to bed now and have a good night's sleep. Things will be better in the morning."

My mother's voice trembled and she managed a smile. "Yes, things will be better in the morning. And *I'm* going to be better. I promise you that, Carla. Things will be different around here from now on. You'll see."

5

CONVERSATION GAP

Although the room was dark when I awoke, I knew it was morning because a finger of pale gray light shone between the closed curtains where they met. When I opened my eyes a little wider I looked at my bedside clock and saw it was eleven o'clock. My throat was raw when I swallowed.

Downstairs, I could hear the vacuum whining and either the television or radio was turned up too loud. A man's voice blatted hysterically away, but whether he was extolling the virtues of a new kind of detergent or announcing the latest news from the "nation's capital," I couldn't tell.

I turned over, burying my face in the pillow. I wished I were back asleep; or, if I could not sleep, that I could stop thinking. Scene after scene shot through my mind, like gigantic colored slides projected on a great white screen. I saw my mother as she'd looked when I'd found her when I'd come home from Glenna Eagles' the night before. I could see her clambering after me, beseeching me, as I'd run ahead of her down the stairs. There was the close-up of her stricken face as I'd pushed her from me so I could escape into the night. Yet the pitiable relief it reflected when I'd returned, tore at me more fiercely still.

Those were my mother's "scenes." But what about *me*? Was *I* so perfect? Had *I* done right? I did not want to think about that.

I got out of bed, slipped down the hall to the bathroom. I showered, brushed my teeth, and stared at myself in the mirror. I looked the same as always. If I'd done anything really wrong when I was out with Dex, wouldn't there be some sign? Or, if there was not a sign, would not a trace of something show?

"I haven't done anything to be ashamed of." I said the words aloud, a little defiantly. The face in the mirror looked righteous. If my mother asked me where I'd been and what I'd been doing, I'd tell her. That was all. I'd say that I ran into a boy I knew . . . *ran* into . . . that was funny . . . and he took me to a friend's house . . . house sounded better than apartment . . . for a little while.

The best thing about the explanation was, of course, that it was the truth. Every single thing that had happened was my mother's fault. I felt tears welling in my eyes. All the dreams I'd dreamed about Tom calling me for a date, all the dreams about the good times we'd have together—even about having a boy for a friend—had been ground down like a small plant that is destroyed before it has a chance to grow. Even if I could find the words to explain to Tom what had happened—it had to be he who'd called, not a single boy had called me about anything since I'd started going to Cedar City High—I'd be too embarrassed to try.

Usually, on Saturdays I lie around for hours wearing my old quilted robe and my Belgian hare slippers, but this Saturday was different. Not until I'd seen my mother and another set of apologies was offered and accepted, tears shed and dried, and fresh promises made could we plan the next step. I didn't know exactly what the next step would be but I did know my mother needed help from somebody—our family doctor or a psychiatrist—and that I had a problem I could no longer cope with alone.

I went back to my room, dressed, made my bed, and ti-

died the top of my desk and dresser. My torn stockings I
wadded into a ball and threw in the wastebasket. I put my
skirt in the back of my closet to be dealt with later. Dexter's sweater was still hanging on the back of the chair
where I'd placed it the night before. I folded it, then stood
wondering what to do with it. Although it seemed silly to
hide it—my mother couldn't have helped noticing I had it
on when I came home—it seemed equally silly to leave
anything lying about that would excite comment, invite
questions, or otherwise divert attention from the matter at
hand. The most sensible thing to do was get it out of the
house as soon as possible, but that couldn't be done before
Monday. Then, however, I could sandwich it in between a
pile of books when I went to school. I'd find out from the
office where Dex's locker was, wait there after class and
give it to him. And that would be the end of that chapter.

I shivered. Last night I'd not had any qualms of con-
science at all, but now that it was morning I didn't much
want to think about Jason de Pleine's apartment in "The
Lotus." Actually, if it had not been for the evidence of the
raw, red scrape on my right knee and the blue sweater I
held in my hands, I might have tried to con-
vince myself that what had happened after I left home had
not happened at all. It really had been queer. Dexter, Chip
and Stomper, Lisl and Daisey Benson sitting around in
that dim, spooky blue light smoking marijuana cigarettes.
And the policeman stopping Dexter and questioning him.
If Dexter had been arrested, they would have taken me
along, too.

I got a funny, all-gone feeling in the pit of my stomach.
Even if the conversation at "The Lotus" had been interesting, even if the kids had accepted me, all the interesting conversation and instant camaraderie in the world
wasn't going to change the fact that smoking marijuana
was against the law. As I thought about it, the sweetish,

smoky smell that had pervaded Jason de Pleine's apartment seemed to come back to me. Then I realized that it was coming from Dexter's sweater which I still held in my hand. Hurriedly, I hid it in the bottom drawer of my dresser under a pile of summer clothes, then went out to listen in the hall. The vacuum was no longer running and the radio was silent.

Back in my room, I lay down on my bed and started to read *I Capture the Castle* which I can nearly always lose myself in though I've read it about fifty times. But it wasn't any use. If my mother wasn't going to come where I was, I'd go to her. I went downstairs.

In the kitchen, I found a note, written on the back of an envelope and propped against the sugar bowl. "Carla, dear: Have gone to store. Be sure and eat some breakfast." That was all. It was no different from dozens of other notes that I'd found on as many Saturday mornings when I'd slept late.

There was orange juice in a container in the refrigerator. I had some of that and then, although I wasn't hungry, I fixed a dish of cold cereal and milk. I took a few bites and was rinsing out the rest in the kitchen sink when I heard my mother's car in the drive.

From the window I could see her as she came toward the house, a big sack of groceries in each arm. She had a bright, green scarf with white polka dots tied around her head but it did not keep a few bright strands of hair from escaping. Her cheeks and the tip of her nose were pink from the cold and she looked very pretty. Seeing her reminded me of that sentence you sometimes see in the front of books: "The characters in this book are fictitious and any resemblance between them and any persons living or dead is purely coincidental." Maybe it was like this with my mother. Maybe one of her selves was real and the other fictitious. But which was which I didn't know.

I opened the back door and took one of the sacks. My mother put the other one down on the table. "It's going to snow," she said brightly. "It's spitting a little right now, and I'm glad. We haven't had a really good snow this winter." She looked in one of the grocery sacks and started taking things out and putting them away.

My throat grew dry. Maybe when she'd finished what she was doing, we would talk about what we were going to do. But she didn't. Neither then, nor all that day. By the next morning I knew she wasn't going to at all.

On Monday, I took Dexter's sweater to school. My mother was in the basement washing and didn't see me go.

At noon I went to the office—I'd told Glenna I was skipping lunch to study, which was partially the truth—and found out that Dexter's locker was almost in the exact position of my own, only in the west wing of the building. It was just about as far away from mine as it could be. Still, I didn't want to carry the sweater around with me all that afternoon so I waited until my last class was over before going to get it. By then, the corridors were swarming with kids and as running is prohibited, almost ten minutes elapsed before I got where I was going.

Dexter wasn't there.

When a small, slight boy who looked as if he ought to be in the sixth grade instead of senior high, slammed his locker door shut I asked him if he'd seen Dexter Smith around.

"Never heard of him."

"He's a senior," I said, lamely.

The kid smirked. "Big deal," he said, and walked away.

Two other boys I asked the same question just said "no."

I moved a few feet away and pretended to read some signs pinned to a bulletin board while I decided whether or not to wait longer. While I was standing there, Marcie Hamilton came charging around the corner toward me. She braked, then stopped.

"Hey, what are you doing way over here? Your locker's on the other side."

"I know," I said. "I'm just waiting for somebody." I tried to shift my books, hoping to conceal the sweater, although I was sure Marcie had already spotted it. She had.

"That looks like Dexter Smith's sweater."

"It is. He loaned it to me."

"Do you date him?"

Although Marcie's question was blunt, her face was so open and cheerful I didn't mind answering. "Not really, I was just out with him one time."

"I used to date him. But we broke up. I still like him, but my folks didn't like him much. He . . ." She paused. "I don't like to say. Besides, you probably know anyway."

I shook my head.

"If you're not dating him it doesn't matter. And, in any case, he's not in school today. I'm in two of his classes and he wasn't there for either one."

She opened her locker which was three or four doors down from Dexter's, then leaped forward with both hands to catch the avalanche of books, loose papers, and assorted wearing apparel that poured out. Not the least perturbed, she started to stuff practically all of it back in the locker. "I'd take you home, but I've got to go to the dentist. Worse luck!"

I said, "Thanks anyway," and was halfway down the corridor when Marcie came scampering after me. "Hey, I almost forgot. I've got a compliment for you. It's from my brother's friend, Tom Willard. You met him at my house the night of the party."

I said I remembered.

"He liked you a lot. He told my brother and my brother

told me. He said you were the first real girl he'd met in ever so."

"I liked him, too. That's why what happened was so awful."

"What happened? Tell me." Marcie moved closer.

"I'll tell you another time," I said, wishing I'd not said anything at all. "Besides, you'll be late to the dentist."

"I'm not in that big a hurry."

There was nothing for me to do but invent the best tale I could. "Tom called me the other night, only there wasn't anybody home except this sort of an aunt of my father. She's old and sort of absentminded and after she'd answered the phone she went to get pencil and paper to write down the telephone number . . ."

Marcie reacted before I could finish. "Oh, no! Don't *tell* me! She wrote down the wrong number!"

"Worst than that. She never came back. In any case when I got home there was the receiver off the hook, just sitting there." The unrehearsed lie had come off so much better than I had expected that I went on with the truth, saying that I didn't even know where Tom was living since his parents had moved out of town and that I couldn't call him to explain even if I did get up the nerve.

"It's not all that hopeless," Marcie said. "I'll write Dave. He goes to State you know, and just happened to be home the weekend of my party. But he'll know how to get in touch with Tom. I'll either call you or tell you at school as soon as I find out."

Walking home, I felt almost happy. If Marcie had accepted my story about a queer, absentminded old aunt answering the telephone, Tom Willard—if I ever saw or heard from him again—might accept it, too.

Then, as if this were a sign, things began to get better. Not perfect, but better. One thing that helped was that my father got a promotion. Not only was he going to make more money, but instead of traveling all the time selling "Tingle" franchises to bottling companies all over the United States, Mr. J. W. Dowitcher wanted him to spend at least one week out of every month in the company's main offices in Cedar City.

The night my father called long distance with the news, my mother was ecstatic. First she talked to him, then I did, then she talked again.

All that week while we were waiting for him to come home, she laughed a lot. I'd never seen her so gay or so full of plans. Most surprising of all, she tried out for a part in *The King and I,* which was the next Little Theater Play. She never would have tried out at all if it hadn't been for her friend, Pam Newquist. Pam was trying out for the part of Anna and suggested my mother go along just to watch.

"Imagine!" my mother said. "I was just sitting there when the director said, 'You there, in the third row, with the pretty hair, *you* read Anna.' Why, I didn't even know he meant me until someone next to me said, 'Go on. He means you.'" She flushed prettily as she told me about it. "Of course, I won't get it—goodness, I've not been in a play since I was in the senior class play in high school—though everyone said I was awfully good in that—but if I should, with all the rehearsals and everything, it would give me something interesting to do on a lot of those evenings when your father is out of town."

I didn't think my mother would get the part, either, but it made her happy to talk about it. So between the play and the knowledge that my father would be home a lot more, the cheerfulness quotient at our house went up about fifty percent. The house was cleaned from top to bottom. Colisimo Q. Quickhart, the neighborhood odd-jobs man who sulks if his employers don't call him Mr.

Quickhart, was called in to wash the windows inside and out, and clean the basement and garage. And my mother laid in stacks of fancy groceries.

In the meantime, Marcie told me she'd written her brother to find out how to get in touch with Tom Willard, but he hadn't answered. This was all right with me. I still hadn't perfected the story I was going to tell. This was the way things stood on Thursday, the day before my father was supposed to get home, when my mother's friend Peg Dendiven dropped in on her way home from shopping.

Peg—she insists I call her that though she's older than my mother and her children are grown—is plump, has shiny black hair that she wears in a tower, and snappy brown eyes. I like her.

"I just heard the good news about Carl," Peg said. She kicked off her pumps and sank down in a chair. "So I thought I'd drop by and help you celebrate. That is, if you'll give me something to celebrate with. Like a small Scotch and water."

"Oh, Peg! Excuse me for not offering you one," my mother said. "I drink so little that I sometimes forget my duties as a hostess."

Peg said, "Forgiven," and waved my mother off to the kitchen with a hand covered with a lot of big chunky rings. To me, she said, "How's the rat race?"

I grinned. I knew she meant school. "Hard. I'm one of those who has to study pretty hard to get good grades. Physics, particularly."

"Physics." Peg made a face. "Thirty years ago it was almost my undoing. In fact, I don't think I would have passed the course if I hadn't given the teacher, who was a rock-hound, the prize geode in my brother's collection."

I asked Peg what a geode was and by the time she'd explained it was a stone that has a cavity lined with crystals, my mother had come back with Peg's drink.

"You're not joining me?" Peg raised an inquisitive eye-brow.

My mother laughed lightly. "We've loads of Scotch, bourbon, and gin—that's what Carl likes for his martinis—but not a drop of vodka. It's the only thing I like." She grimaced. "The others, I can't stand the taste."

Peg grinned. "Tough luck. I like 'em all. But you," she added, turning to me, "you stay away from all of them, hear?"

"Don't worry, I will." When my mother laughed too brightly, I realized I'd spoken with more vehemence than I'd intended. I hung around a few more minutes then asked to be excused. I said that in addition to tons of homework, I'd promised to make a poster for the Art Fair at school.

Gesturing with a lighted cigarette, Peg told me to run along. "You come and visit me someday," she said, "all by your lonesome."

I said that someday I would, and made my escape. The conversation—my mother saying she really didn't drink very much and Peg, who obviously knew that she did, asking me to come and see her—had made me nervous. Not until the next morning, however, when I went to the basement to look for some construction paper before going to school, did I know how much I had to be nervous about.

In the process of looking for the paper, I found a bunch of stuff I'd nearly forgotten about in a storage cupboard off the laundry room. There were boxes of neatly labeled boxes of baby clothes and drawings my sister and I had made that dated back to kindergarten. I was touched that my mother had saved them all. I found our Lincoln Logs—Di and I had really loved those—and a big box full of games. The next thing I found was the vodka, a cache of it lying on its side in a shadowy corner.

I just stood there staring until my mother called down to ask what in the world I was doing, and to add rather sharply that if I didn't hurry I would be late to school.

I shut the cupboard door and without looking any further for the paper, went upstairs.

"Of course, you can talk to me," my father said, heartily. "Come in, come in! We're going to have to make a practice of regular talks."

Quietly, I shut the study door behind me. "I don't want mother to know."

My father pretended alarm. "Have I forgotten something? Birthday, wedding anniversary? It's too early for Christmas." He flipped the pages of his desk calendar and laughed. "What's the deal, doll?"

I shook my head. "It's not anything like that." I moved into his study and sat down on the edge of the chair nearest him. My father's week at home was almost up and I still hadn't figured out how to tell him about finding all that vodka right after my mother had said she hadn't any in the house.

My father looked at me so closely that I moved uneasily. His face clouded. "You . . . you're not in any kind of trouble?" Though his voice was gruff it was gentle, too.

I nodded, then began to cry. "It's Mama. . . ."

"Mama!" My father's cheeks puffed out as he exploded the word, then he shook his head. He said, "Mama," again, and reaching for his handkerchief he laughed until tears came to his eyes. "When you started talking, I thought you were in trouble with a boy." He paused, gave me a guilty look and started correcting himself. "I'm sorry, Carla. I didn't mean that. But you know, just for a moment there . . ."

"It's all right," I said. It wasn't, but once we had started

61

talking I couldn't afford to let my feelings get in the way. I blundered on. "It *is* Mama. She's drinking. . . ."

"Drinking!" The word burst forth from my father's lips the same way he'd said, "Mama!" This time, he didn't laugh but I think he wanted to. "Go on," he said. His face was pink.

"Drinking too much."

"You're talking preposterous nonsense," my father said. For him the conversation wasn't funny any more. "Of course, your mother has a cocktail now and then, a social drink with friends, but she's not had even that since I've been home."

"But it's the truth." I no longer cared about being tactful. "She doesn't drink much when you're here. Only when you're away—and I'm away. Last Thursday, she told Peg Dendiven she didn't have any vodka in the house—that was why she couldn't drink with her. Yet the very next morning when I was looking for some construction paper in the basement, I found some she'd hidden."

"Show me," my father said. He pushed back his chair so angrily he had to grab it so it wouldn't tip over.

He moved toward the door and I followed. I felt as if my body was inhabited by somebody else. In the bathroom across the hall I could still hear water running in the shower. My mother always takes a long time to get ready when she and my father are going out.

My father had already gone ahead of me down the stairs and flipped on the basement light. He had not spoken since we left the study. With long steps he moved into the storage room and flung open the cupboard doors. "There's no liquor here," he said flatly. "I knew there wouldn't be."

"But there was!" My tongue was thick, and I felt lightheaded and ill. "Vodka. I don't know how many bottles . . . four or five . . . on the top shelf behind the construction paper."

"See for yourself."

I looked and there was nothing there.

My father put his arm around my shoulder, gave it a light reassuring squeeze. "You were confused, that's all. So let's not say any more about it. O.K.? We'll just forget the whole thing."

I didn't answer. There wasn't anything I could say. Pleading a headache, I went to my room and stayed there until after my father and mother had left for their party. Then I went downstairs to call Diane.

"Kappa Rho House!" The words were trilled invitingly.

"I'd like to speak to Diane Devon."

"Just a minute, I'll see if she's still here."

I moved the receiver from my right hand to my left, drying the sweaty palms against the side of my slacks. Still listening I could hear the echoing voice of the girl who had answered calling, "Di! Diane Devon, wanted on the phone! I think it's long distance."

If Diane was there, it was taking longer to get her to the telephone than I'd expected. It was costing more, too. But not until my mother got the phone bill would I have to worry about an explanation.

"Hello, this is Diane." My sister's voice was breathless, a little impatient.

"This is Carla . . . I called up," I said pointlessly.

"Oh." Diane sounded surprised, then a second later anxious. "Is . . . is something wrong? Mother . . . Daddy . . . an accident?"

"No. Not an accident, but . . ."

Though I paused only for a second, fumbling for words, Diane intervened before I could go on. "Then it's nothing serious, is it? Why don't you *write* me and tell me all about it? That would be *much* the best thing to do. Then, I'll write you back the very next day. I promise."

"I have to talk to you now," I said. Even before the connection was broken, I could feel her beginning to slip away from me. I let the words pour forth. "It's about Mother. She's drinking too much . . . hiding bottles of vodka around the house . . . alcoholics do that . . . I told Daddy and he doesn't believe me!" My voice rose hysterically and then trailed off leaving a silence; then my heart began to pound. "I . . . I don't know what to do . . . Di! Answer me? Are you still there . . . ?"

"I'm here," Diane said. "I'm just trying to figure out what to say to you. I guess I thought you . . . knew. But, in any case, you know now."

"What am I going to do?" I began to whimper.

Again there was a little silence and when Diane spoke again the impatience I'd been sensing since we'd started to talk was undisguised.

"I'd help you, if I could, but right now I've got some problems of my own. Maybe after I get them straightened out . . . I can come home for a weekend. In the meantime, you write me, like I said. O.K.?"

I said, "O.K." but by then Diane had hung up.

6

THE GOLDEN FLEECE

Monday afternoon when I got home from school there was a strange car parked in front of our house. If we had visitors, I didn't want to see them no matter who they were. To be on the safe side, I let myself in by the back door, only to discover there wasn't anybody there except my mother and father, who were drinking coffee in the kitchen.

My mother smiled. "We've been waiting for you, dear. Sit down and have a little something to eat."

As she spoke, my father got up and pushed back a chair for me but I shook my head. "Thanks. Maybe a little later. I've had this sort of headache all day."

"Daddy won't be here later," my mother said. "I'm going to take him to the airport in just a little bit. Besides, your head will feel better if you eat something."

After I sat down, she poured a glass of milk and set it before me with three cookies on a paper napkin. Over my head I could see her exchanging glances with my father. "Oh, Carl. Let's tell her. I just can't stand to put it off another minute."

"Don't tell me Daddy's got another promotion?" I meant the question ironically, money being the only thing that seemed to matter around our house. But I really did have a headache and the words came out nastier than I'd intended. As it turned out, however, it didn't matter. My mother and father were both so wrapped up in their little game they paid no attention.

My father was looking pleased. "When a company or corporation does well, it declares a dividend to its stockholders. So I'm declaring a little dividend to *my* stockholders. You, Mama, and Diane." As he spoke, he reached in his pocket and tossed a key chain with two small keys suspended from it across the table toward me. "*Your* dividend is out in front."

I looked at the keys but I didn't pick them up. "I . . . I don't know what you mean."

"You saw the blue car in front of the house?"

I nodded. "I thought we had company—that's why I came in the back door."

My mother jumped up and hugged me from behind. "Oh, Carla! It's yours! Daddy's giving it to you! A car of your very own! Diane, too. She can't have a car on campus until she's a senior, but Daddy's giving her the money for it now so everything will be completely fair."

"I don't know what to say." I looked from one happy, expectant face to the other and knew that wasn't enough. They either wanted me to say something or else jump up and down, exclaim, hug and kiss them.

"Diane just can't get over it," my mother said by way of contrast. "Daddy talked to her at the sorority house just a little while ago. When he told her he was putting three thousand dollars in her account, you'd never guess what she did." Without waiting for me to reply, she supplied the answer. "Cried! Daddy had to put me on the phone to talk to her until she calmed down a little."

"I'm too stunned to cry," I said and at last I must have got it right for my parents both began to laugh.

"Too stunned to cry!" my father repeated. "Too stunned even to ask what make it is! But I understand that. If anybody had given me a car when I was sixteen, even an old jalopy, I would probably have dropped dead. Put your coat back on and we'll go have a turn around the block. Don't forget the key."

"And don't be gone more than a few minutes," my mother called after us. "We've barely time to get to the airport as it is."

My father took my arm as we cut across the lawn to the blue car. The wind whipped away his words as he spoke. "It's a Mustang. I thought you'd like that. I've got you insured for everything in the book." He laughed. "Insurance cost almost as much as the car!"

He opened the door on the driver's side to let me in, then got in himself. The car was beautiful inside. The upholstery was just a little bit lighter blue than the body and it had a new car smell. My father was purposely quiet so I would not be nervous as I got it started and turned down the street. The snow that my mother had predicted but which had never materialized, began to fall in earnest and my father reached across me and turned on the windshield wiper when I couldn't find the right knob on the strange dashboard. The car drove easily and the motor was so quiet that the regular "whup whup" of the windshield wipers was the only sound. At that moment, I loved my father very much and I felt that if we might only keep on driving into that silent, sifting whiteness as darkness fell that we might be able to talk to each other. But when he looked at his watch I knew it was time to turn back. Months passed before we had a chance to talk again.

When I told Marcie about my car, she staggered and pretended she was about to fall. The occasion, however, wasn't really all that happy. That was the day she came around after school to tell me that Tom Willard's telephone number would have to remain a mystery until her brother came home again from college.

"Dave said he wrote the number down inside the front cover of the phone book. But there are already so many telephone numbers written on that page that you'd need an expert to decipher them. I asked my mother if I could just tear the whole page out and send it to Dave so he could identify it. But she won't let me. She's got a lot of her own favorite numbers on that page."

I said it didn't matter. And it really didn't. Losing Tom seemed to be part of the pattern of my life. Just like getting a car of my own should have made me happy, yet somehow seemed to have had just the opposite effect.

Marcie, who was standing beside my locker as we talked, watched as I hauled out the books I planned to take home. "Hey," she said, "you've still got Dexter's sweater in there."

As it was in plain sight, I couldn't deny it. "I hardly ever see him. And I don't like hanging around his locker."

"I'll give it to him," Marcie said. "It wouldn't be any trouble for me, at all."

When I replied that I thought I ought to return what I had borrowed, Marcie only grinned and trotted off.

After she had left, I took the sweater down from the shelf, sniffed at it, and put it back knowing that I probably should have let Marcie give it to him. But the truth of it was that I liked having the sweater in my locker. I liked its softness, the faint smoky-sweet smell. I liked Dex and it amused me that Marcie Hamilton did, too.

It was almost dark when I got home. First I'd taken Glenna for a ride to show off the car and then when we got to her house four little Eagles came swarming out and I had to take them around the block.

Lights were on all up and down the street. In some of the houses the draperies had not yet been drawn and I could see mothers, fathers, and children moving about like actors on a stage. Firelight gleamed.

My own house was dark. I tried to remember if my mother had said anything about playing bridge that day but communication between us was, at best, imperfect. If her car wasn't in the garage I could assume she'd be along presently, either buoyed up by winning two or three dollars or depressed to a similar degree.

But when I put my car away, her car was there, too. With the taste of fear in my mouth, I ran toward the house.

My mother was sleeping when I found her. A glass and an empty vodka bottle were on the bedside table. The letter from Diane lay crumpled on the floor.

It was very short. And though I haven't seen the letter since, I can still see the way the words looked on the page, see Diane's writing—usually so careful—slanting up hill as if she'd written in much haste.

"Dear Mama and Daddy," I read. "Please don't hate me and forgive me if you can. The three thousand dollars Daddy deposited in my account here at school was an answer to a prayer. Nick and I were married this morning. I will write you when I can. Love, Diane."

There was a postscript. "By the time you get this letter, Nick and I will be on our way to California."

I slipped off my mother's shoes and covered her with the throw from the chaise, but although she stirred she did not waken. I snapped off the light that I'd turned on when I came into the room and went downstairs and moved through the silent house. An unopened pile of mail, including a letter from my Aunt Esther, my mother's favorite older sister, lay on a table in the front hall. In the kitchen, a cup of cold coffee and a half-smoked cigarette were on the counter. Mechanically, I rinsed out the cup and emptied the ash tray. Had I been home that morning I could not have seen more clearly what happened. After she'd opened Diane's letter, she'd never returned to finish her coffee or read other mail that ordinarily would have been of interest to her. She had taken the vodka from its new hiding place—how clever she had been to take it out of the basement cupboard so my father wouldn't find it there—and had settled quietly down to forget as best she could the grief and disappointment that Diane's letter brought. It was hard for me to understand how she felt about Diane, yet in a way I did understand it. She'd pinned so many hopes on Di. Now all her hopes were gone and Diane with them.

I tried to think about Diane being married. Married to somebody named Nick whose last name I didn't even know. Nothing would ever be the same again between us. A week before when I'd talked to Diane on the phone, I'd felt her slipping away from me. Knowing the reason only increased the void in my life. Diane had someone to love and being loved, she had escaped. I had nobody. For me, there was no escape at all.

I was so wrapped in misery when the phone rang that I answered it only because I was afraid the noise would waken my mother before I was prepared to face her.

A moment's silence followed my quavered hello, then a boy's voice said uncertainly, "I'm calling Carla Devon. Is she there?"

I stood, holding the receiver against my chest with one hand, wiping my tear-smeared eyes and face with my other sweatered arm before managing a reply so unintelligible that another silence followed before the boy spoke again, this time apologetically. "This is Dexter Smith. But I'm afraid . . . it doesn't sound as if I'm calling at too good a time. I'll give you a ring sometime."

"I . . . I want to talk."

"If you're sure . . ." His voice was still uncertain.

"I want to . . . but I'm afraid if I do I'm going to cry."

"That won't get you anyplace." He sounded cool, almost reproving. "Crying is for squares. You just sit tight and I'll come and get you—that is if you think you can get away."

"I can get away," I said. "Nobody here even knows I'm home."

"That figures," Dexter said. He was laughing softly as the receiver clicked.

I looked at my mother before I left. She was still sleeping. I picked up the empty vodka bottle to take it to the kitchen, then with a little smile put it back on the table beside her. If crying was for squares, so was sympathy. I wanted that empty bottle to be the first thing she saw when she awoke.

I was waiting outside in the shadows when I saw Dexter's car coming down the street. He cut off his headlights before he swung into the drive. When he saw me running across the lawn toward him, he opened the door but did not speak until we had turned off our street and onto the parkway. "Both times we've met," he said, "the conditions have seemed to be remarkably the same. Right?"

I nodded.

"Maybe you think there isn't anything you can do about it. Right?"

"Right," I sniffled.

Dex shook his head. "That's where you're wrong." Although he was smiling at his little play on words, I could tell he was serious. "It's true you can't change the *conditions* of your life, but you can change your *attitude* toward them so they don't matter so much any more. Do you follow me?"

"I . . . I think so."

"Do you *want* to? Change them, I mean?"

"Why not? I don't see how things can get much worse than they are now." The harsh unfamiliar laugh was mine.

Dex laughed, too, but softly, approvingly. "Well, then.

71

Very good. We'll drop in at 'The Lotus' and see friend Jason. I don't want to twist your arm, you know, but today is pay day. And Jason has a new supply—of Golden Fleece."

We got no answer when we rang the bell so Dex used his own key to let us into the building and then into Jason's apartment. It was lighted as before: a string of small blue bulbs outlining the ceiling; the same rotating colored lights forming shifting patterns on the walls. A Bob Dylan record was turned on very low.

"He must have gone out to eat or something." Dex seemed to be talking not to me but to himself. "In any case, he'll have left it for me."

Not wanting to be alone, I followed when Dexter pushed through a swinging door into the kitchen. Then I wished I hadn't. The sink was full of coffee grounds, the scrapings of burned toast, and dirty dishes. A pan on the stove held the hardened remains of some kind of cooked cereal. I'd seen bugs scuttling out of sight as Dexter turned on the bright overhead light and a few bug bodies lay mashed here and there on the floor.

When Dex opened the refrigerator, I peered in, too. It seemed to hold nothing but a bottle of clabbered milk, a banana turned black with age, and a small box. I thought, "Uck," but Dexter looked pleased. Clearing a place on the counter, he opened the box which I could now see had his name written on it with a marking pencil, and took out a plastic bag. He spilled a few tobaccoish-looking crumbs from the bag into the palm of his hand. "All manicured and ready to go. I'd say there's enough for at least thirty-five or forty sticks. Beautiful! Come on, I'll show you what we do next. See if you can find a spoon in that drawer."

I found a teaspoon, not too clean-looking, washed it and dried it on a paper napkin. Dex had gone back into the living room, shoved a bunch of magazines and newspapers off the coffee table and turned on a floor lamp that seemed to contain a perfectly ordinary hundred-watt bulb. He sat down on the floor in front of the coffee table and I squatted down beside him.

"When I say it's 'manicured,' that means it's not full of stems and coarse pieces that you have to go through and pick out before you can start making your sticks. The stuff that grows around here in the summertime is no good at all. A couple of years ago, a bunch of kids from the East who'd heard that marijuana was growing wild all over the place, came out here thinking they'd make a killing. You know, harvest bales of the stuff, roast it in their ovens at home, and then sell it to their pot-hungry friends at a big profit. Unfortunately, they were careless and before they could find out that the stuff wasn't any good, the fuzz got them—but good."

I laughed because Dexter did.

"But Jason," he continued, "on the other hand, nearly always gets *good* stuff. That's why the kids are willing to pay a decent price." From his pocket he took a little folder of cigarette papers, sluffed off a dozen or so of them and placed them side by side on the coffee table. "The pot goes on next. You take that spoon, fill it just about so"—he showed me—"and sprinkle it down the middle of each paper like this, then we'll roll them. There's a kind of a trick to that." Again he illustrated, holding the cigarette paper with the fingers of both hands and gently shaking the marijuana until it was distributed almost the entire length of the paper. Expertly, he rolled it up, ran his tongue along the edge to seal it and tucked in both ends.

It looked rather limp to me, and also shorter and thinner than a regular cigarette but Dexter regarded it with satisfaction. He put it in his mouth, then took it out again. "Business before pleasure. With you helping me, it shouldn't take too long."

For a while, I just measured the marijuana out on the papers and let Dex roll, but my job took less time than his and when he got too far behind he said I could try rolling. I couldn't get the hang of it though and we went back to what we'd been doing in the beginning.

It took us over an hour to make forty-two cigarettes, but it didn't seem that long. We talked a lot. I told Dex that the night he almost ran over me, I was running away because I'd come home and found my mother drunk. And that tonight when he'd called, it had happened again because my sister had run away and got married. I'd never used the word "drunk" before in referring to my mother, but saying it, facing up to the fact that that is what she was, made me feel better.

Dexter did not seem surprised. "I thought it was probably something like that. I'm just glad that both times I happened to be around." He added that our second meeting, actually, had been just as much a matter of chance as the first. He'd even forgotten I had his sweater until he bumped into Marcie right after she'd seen it in my locker. She'd told him that I was sort of worried about returning it. "That's why I called you tonight. To tell you not to worry, to keep it if you wanted to. I've got at least forty more. That's the only thing my mother can ever think of to send me for Christmas."

I said I'd like to keep it and he said, "It's yours."

By this time we were almost through. Dexter looked to see how much marijuana was left in the plastic bag, then told me to divide it all between four papers. When they were rolled they were almost twice as fat as the ones we'd been making. Dexter called them "dirigibles" and said they were for us.

He turned off the floor lamp, letting the swirling colored lights take over again, then reached for my hand and led me across the room to the place we'd sat before and fixed pillows behind our backs.

"Comfortable?"

It was so dark I could hardly see his face but I knew he was smiling. I nodded.

A match spurted, its flame glowing briefly as he lighted one of the dirigibles and handed it to me. I inhaled deeply, but I did not cough or choke as I thought I might do.

"Again," Dexter said softly. "Hold it as long as you can." He waited, then said, "Now again."

He took it from me, inhaled, held, and passed it back to me. I cupped my hands around it, inhaled, feeling the heat on my face. "You keep it," Dexter said, "until I prepare our filter tip." I knew he was making a joke, but I did not know what it was until I saw him strip the remaining matches out of a book of safety matches and roll the empty folder around the unlighted end to make a mouthpiece. "When it gets too hot you can hold it on a pin, but I like this way better." He then said, "Finish it," and I did.

I leaned back against the cushions, knowing that Dexter was watching me closely, knowing that he sat less than a foot away from me. Yet, if this was so, why did his head seem to be bobbing around near the ceiling as if it were a balloon on the end of a string. Such a phenomenon should have been alarming, but it did not seem that way at all. It just happened to be the way it was. I told Dex what his head was doing and he laughed harder than I did.

He lighted another cigarette and moved closer to me. His arm was around my shoulders but it was light and pressureless. "I don't need to ask if you're happy. I can tell. The problem is, if you're going to *stay* happy and you have to *work* at it, see? You have to learn to *cool* it. Cooling it is the big thing. You have to get high, see, and not have anyone know it. You have to cool it, stay cool and look out the window at all the stupid people rat-racing around, working at their pointless jobs, discriminating against their neighbors . . ."

"Giving themselves airs . . ."

"And, in general making you as unhappy as they are themselves."

From people in general, we went on to society, then back to our parents, teachers, and all the "squares" we knew.

Dex really had the answers. I felt as if I, too, was beginning to see things clearly for the first time. But best of all, I liked "cooling it." I *liked* looking out the window. At everybody.

7

THE DOUBLE LIFE OF CARLA DEVON

The first thing I learned to do was become a good liar. "Learned," however, isn't really the right word. I didn't learn how to lie, it just came to me. The funny thing is, that I'd always been so terrible at it before. Perhaps, because I'd had so little practice. And, of course, there had been no necessity.

Now I lied whether I needed to or not. For example, I wouldn't have needed to explain why I was so often late getting home from school. If a girl was *in* lots of things and had lots of friends, she would just naturally be late getting home. My mother believed that because that is the way Diane had been.

So when I told my mother I was on this committee making plans for Brotherhood Week—I wasn't on the committee, but Glenna was—she wanted to believe me. At least, it took her mind off Diane for a few minutes and that was worth a lot.

We'd only had a postcard in the three weeks since the letter arrived that said she was married. The postcard, postmarked Salt Lake City, showed a picture of the tomb of Brigham Young and told about him founding the Mormon Church. Diane, herself, had only written a few lines. Something about how many miles they'd driven that day and ending "We're both divinely happy. Nick sends his love."

"You don't suppose he's a Mormon, do you?" my mother said. We were eating dinner in the kitchen as we always did when my father wasn't home. For about the thousandth time she picked up the card and stared at it as if by severe concentration she could extract something more from either the message or the picture. "With the name 'Nick' I had thought he probably was an Italian. But now I don't know. A person wouldn't have to go to California by way of Salt Lake City unless he particularly wanted to go there."

"He might," I said. "Lots of people go to California by way of Salt Lake City who aren't anything. They go that way because it's the shortest. Or because they want to see the lake. Or see that temple that's built without any nails. I've read that you can drop a pin in there and hear it all over the place. *I'd* like to go to Salt Lake City and I'm not a Mormon."

"If we knew his last name that would help a little."

Although my mother seemed relieved that Nick might not be a Mormon, it presented her with another worry she'd not expressed before. "If he's an Italian, he's probably a Catholic. If he is . . ." Her voice quavered. "If he's a Catholic, there'll be all kinds of problems."

"But maybe he isn't. With a name like Nick," I said, "maybe he's Greek. Maybe he's a member of the Greek Orthodox Church and if he is they may go live in Athens. But whatever he is, it doesn't matter. Diane is married to him. For all we know he may be a white, Anglo-Saxon Protestant. With blue eyes."

"To think that Diane could have married *anybody*. There was that nice Hitchcock boy who came all the way from New Jersey last summer to see her. His family had their own plane. He was crazy about her. She would have had everything if she'd married him."

"I know," I said. "But she didn't. She married Nick.

She loves him. The only reason she ran off and got married is because she knew you'd carry on just like you're carrying on. After things have had time to settle down, you'll have a long letter from her telling you about everything. And when you've really forgiven her, she'll bring Nick home."

My mother wiped her eyes. "I just think I'll call your father. He'll be home tomorrow night, but still I'd like to talk to him. I can reach him now at his hotel."

"If that will make you feel better," I said, "though you might want to wait until after Dexter and I have left."

My mother put down her fork. "Dexter? Dexter who?"

"Dexter Smith." My mother was so pathetically interested I was almost sorry I hadn't told her sooner I had a date. "We're going to a party one of the kids at school is giving. A girl named Lisl Camp."

Almost before I'd finished speaking my mother started clearing the table. "You might want to bring Dexter in for something to eat afterward. I could make a pot of cocoa and just leave it on the stove . . ."

"Don't bother." I brushed my cheek against my mother's. I was really feeling quite kindly toward her. "We'll probably have eaten tons of stuff at Lisl's and not want any more."

My mother followed me to the stairway as I started up to get ready. "I've heard of the Camp Construction Company. They build dams and bridges all over. Would Lisl be the daughter of that Mr. Camp?"

I said she was.

My mother looked quite pleased. "Pam Newquist was telling me just the other day that wherever in the world Mr. Camp goes on business that Mrs. Camp goes with him."

I said that I knew that, too.

While I was getting ready I counted up the times Dexter and I had been together since the night he almost ran over me. You couldn't really call them dates because they'd hardly lasted long enough. Still, I told myself, I'd been the one he asked instead of about a dozen other people who would have jumped at the chance to smoke a marijuana cigarette whatever the circumstances.

Once we'd met before school and shared a stick between us, and three or four times we'd smoked in my car during the lunch hour. Dexter said pot helped him clarify his thoughts and to understand things better. I knew what he meant, though I usually felt just lightheaded and happy—sort of floating about one foot off the floor. One time Mr. Carrington, who teaches math, sprang a surprise test on us and I sat the whole period just looking at the theorem we were supposed to prove, thinking how interesting it was, and not getting anything down on paper at all. When I told Dexter, he said it was because I wasn't experienced enough. If you were going to smoke pot, he said, you had to learn how to discipline yourself when you were taking tests or studying. I'd already discovered you had to be careful when driving—learn to compensate, Dex called it—because distances didn't seem the same.

I liked it better when we went to the park after school. We'd been there three or four times, too. Sometimes we took Dexter's car and sometimes mine, though Dexter always drove. The spot we liked best was the parking lot for the little children's playground, which was up a little hill from the lagoon. In the summer, the place was packed with parents and kids, but in winter there was never anybody up there except an occasional couple sitting there necking.

Dexter was always very careful whenever we sat in the car with the motor running. He'd roll both front windows down a couple of inches so there would be plenty of air circulating. He said the last thing he wanted was to die of carbon monoxide poisoning. But even with the wind blowing through, it was pleasant to sit in the car and watch the ice skaters gliding about on the lagoon. The children wore bright jackets and stocking caps and there was always a dog or two running back and forth barking and spilling the little kids. With the snow all around, and the sun shining it was beautiful. Dexter said everything was more beautiful when you were smoking pot. The funny thing was—and f a while it bothered me—I couldn't remember exactly the way things were when you weren't.

So that was the way things stood until the morning when I found Dexter waiting at my locker when I came to school. Just by looking at him I could tell he was straight and not just because he didn't have on his dark glasses. (As soon as I'd discovered that smoking pot made the pupils in my eyes as big as marbles, I'd got myself dark glasses, too.) The night of Marcie Hamilton's party I hadn't even known what the word "straight" meant!

"Pot party tonight at Lisl Camp's," Dex said, happily. "Her folks are out of town and we'll have the whole place to ourselves." He laughed. "Lisl is staying with Betty Dermott while her parents are away, but she's got the key to her own house, of course. We're going to meet over there about eight o'clock. If you'd like to go, I'll pick you up."

"Won't Betty's parents wonder where she and Lisl are?" I'd wondered the thought aloud.

Dexter laughed again. "Nothing to worry about. *They* think the girls are staying all night with Doris Denman, and Doris's parents don't care what time *anybody* gets home." Suddenly, he frowned. "What's it to you, anyway? If you don't like the arrangement you don't need to go."

"But I want to go!" I was really anguished.

"Of course, you do." Dex was smiling again. "That's the power of pot. You just start thinking about it, and all your little scruples go down the drain."

I knew that Dexter was speaking in fun, but it upset me a little, too. Thinking about the light, happy, kind of crazy feeling I got when I was smoking pot was what had made me forget that it wasn't right for Lisl Camp to be having a bunch of kids in her house when her parents were out of town.

I heard Dexter's car in the drive, and for the second time that day I pushed the thought from my mind.

My mother had opened the door before I could get downstairs. I noticed that she had changed from the slacks and sweater she'd had on at dinner to the new floor-length wool hostess gown she'd bought to replace the gold corduroy. I'd not seen that one since the night I'd come home from Glenna's house and found her drunk. Like the gold one, this one was made with some kind of fullness in the back. I think she knew it made her look like a princess. She was holding out both hands to Dexter who, I was pleased to see, looked very nice. At least he had not gotten himself up in the rather odd fashion in which he sometimes comes to school.

"You're Dexter Smith," said my mother, then added with a little smile, "Carla's told me all about you."

"She's told me all about you, too, Mrs. Devon." Dexter's manner was both engaging and boyish. I could see my mother was charmed. Certainly, she never suspected just how much Dexter knew.

"Won't you sit down, Dexter? Carla will be down presently."

I said, "I'm down," and my mother said, "Oh, there you are!" as if she'd not noticed me on the stairs a moment before. She sighed prettily. "Well, I suppose you two will want to be running along to your party."

"I'm afraid we have to," Dexter said. Somehow he managed to sound genuinely regretful. "It's nice here, though. Perhaps some other time."

"Anytime," my mother said, following us to the door. "You just come anytime."

In the car Dexter said, "Whew!" and then after a minute. "You didn't tell me she was a knockout."

"I didn't think it was necessary. Sooner or later everyone finds out." I must have sounded sour because Dexter nodded approvingly. "I can see how it would bug you. She bugs me and we aren't even related." He cleared his voice and assuming a ladylike voice that really did sound rather a bit like my mother, sang out, "Ooh! You're Dexter Smith! Carla's told me all about you." Dexter started laughing at himself and pretty soon I was laughing, too. Then as suddenly I stopped. "She's not really that bad," I said. "She . . . she's really very nice. Once when I had a strep throat there was almost a solid week when she didn't go to bed at all. She . . . she does nice things for people. We . . . my sister and I . . . and my mother used to have good times together. It's just that recently . . . I don't know." Without wanting to I was crying.

Dexter drew the car in toward the curbing and stopped. "This isn't going to do at all. If you're going to get affection and sentiment and *facts* all mixed up together you're a loser before you start. Sure, your mother's nice. Your father's a great guy. The same goes for my parents, too. But now the ball's in the other court, see? *Now* it's people between thirty-five and forty-five who are confused. We can figure it out." Dexter handed me his handkerchief. I wiped my eyes and he started the car.

Neither of us said another word until we stopped in front of Lisl Camp's house but all the time I was thinking that what Dexter said really did make sense.

I don't know what I'd expected Lisl's house to be like, but certainly not so enormous. It loomed up against the dark sky like a medieval castle. There were three or four cars in the drive, invisible from the street because of all the big clumps of trees and bushes that skirted it.

Dexter let the knocker fall and less than a second later, Lisl came to the door. She was wearing the same funny outfit she'd had on at Jason de Pleine's apartment—the skinny pants and the poncho arrangement. She wasted no time, though, on greetings. "Have you got it?" Her small, pale face had a sharp eager look.

"Patience, child, patience. Doesn't Uncle Dexter always deliver?" With a flourish, he produced a flat, one-pound candy box from the brown paper bag that he had tucked under his arm. "Enough for everybody and some to spare."

Lisl made a quick grab for the box but Dexter, laughing, held it over her head out of reach. "Oh, no, you don't. This time it's cash on the line. No more owing the company store. Where is everybody, anyway? Downstairs?"

Lisl nodded, then rather crossly said, "Well, come on."

Dexter and I followed Lisl through a large formal living room and dining room into the kitchen. Here there was a great gleaming stove, an enormous refrigerator and freezer, a butcher's block, and what seemed to be miles of counter space. If it hadn't been for all the equipment for preparing and storing food I might never have noticed that there wasn't as much as a potato chip in sight.

A flight of stairs led downward from the kitchen, but not until we were almost at the bottom could I tell that there was any kind of party going on. And certainly, even then, not much of one. In fact, everyone seemed to be sitting around doing nothing. It was exactly the opposite of all the things that had been going on at Marcie Hamilton's house the night I'd first met Dex.

All that changed when Lisl called out, "He's here!" A half a dozen or so kids who'd been arranged around the low-ceilinged, timbered room, got up and came over to meet Dex. Chip and Stomper and Daisey Benson all of whom had been at "The Lotus," were among them. There were also two tall thin boys, who looked like brothers, Betty Dermott—whom I knew only by sight at school—and a girl whose small, wedge-shaped face was almost concealed by a fall of straight dark hair. That, I supposed, was Doris Denman. No one introduced me.

"I hope you've all got some money," Lisl sang out, "because Dexter says no money, no smokee." She giggled, then putting her finger to her lips looked around. "Where do you want to conduct your . . . er . . . business?"

"What about here?" Dexter touched a section of a long, polished bar that stretched across one end of the room.

"Why not?" Lisl shrugged. "Might as well use it for something. My father hasn't left as much as a bottle of beer loose in the house."

Dexter moved behind the bar, motioned me to follow. "In case you don't know it, you're treasurer." Opening the candy box he took out a plastic bag that held, I supposed, the cigarettes we'd made at Jason de Pleine's apartment almost a week before. But as he took them out and lined them up on the bar, I could see that they were much more carefully made. Except for the fact that they were skinnier, they looked like conventional cigarettes.

Dexter read my mind. "The other batch we made up is all gone. Sold some of 'em at school and you and I smoked the rest. This is a new shipment." He picked one up and held it airily in his fingers. "I used part of my profits from the ones we made to buy a cigarette-making machine. I can turn them out, now, faster than you can say 'pot party.' "

Lisl had already grabbed one. "How much?"

"For an old customer," Dexter said, "fifty cents. Though I should get more. I understand that a good stick is getting a dollar lots of places." His hand closed over the two quarters that Lisl had produced from under her poncho. "Does Madame wish to smoke it here or take it with her?"

"Funny boy," Lisl said, not laughing. Again she reached under her poncho, this time placing two crumpled dollar bills on the bar.

"Four sticks coming up," Dexter said in a mock deep voice. He pushed them toward me. "Put them in a sandwich bag for the lady."

For the next fifteen or twenty minutes, business was brisk. Dexter had made forty cigarettes and we sold them all.

I counted the money, putting the bills together with a rubber band and the change in a small box. Dexter pocketed it all, looking pleased. "A good night's work—and the night is scarcely begun."

"But what about us?" I didn't even try to conceal my disappointment. "You shouldn't have sold them all."

Dexter laughed softly. "Silly girl. I'm not that stupid. We're taken care of. Now come along while I tell Lisl we're going on an errand, but that we'll be back."

Lisl, who was sitting on a red leather sofa between the two tall thin brothers, couldn't care less what we planned to do. Already the heavy, heady, sweet-smelling smoke was layering around the room. The party was starting to swing. Someone had turned on the hi-fi. A girl with a throaty voice was singing "Break on Through to the Other Side." Until Dex had told me, I hadn't known that songs like "Break on Through," "Fat Angel," "Candy Man," and a lot of others were about drugs. At first, I didn't believe him. Dex said he didn't know how anybody could be so square. That a lot of recording stars—Donovan, The Mothers of Invention, The Doors, and even The Beatles—all sang about them, too. It made me feel funny to think about all the times I'd heard those songs and hadn't really understood them. Also a little sad. There were some things I didn't like about being "in" at all.

Upstairs, we found our coats and then Dexter fixed the lock on the front door so we could get back in the house later, then taking my hand we ran to the car.

The night was very cold and clear with about a million stars. A Tom Willard night. I twitched my head. I hoped that for the rest of my life I wasn't going to think about Tom Willard every time I saw a bunch of stars.

Dexter flicked a glance in my direction. "Troubles?"

"Just something I don't want to think about."

"There's a cure for that, you know."

"Not now. I'll wait for you. Until we get back to Lisl's."

"With luck, it shouldn't take me long."

"What is it we're . . . you're going to do?"

"Meet a fellow. Actually, I guess there isn't any reason why I shouldn't tell you. After all, you and I are partners—in a way. I'm meeting Jason de Pleine."

"At 'The Lotus'?"

Dexter shook his head. "No, he's not there. I talked to him just before I picked you up and he said he'd be somewhere in the university district. He couldn't say exactly."

Already I could see lying ahead of us the large sprawling campus of Cedar City University. The business district that served it twinkled away to our right. It was this way we turned, Dexter letting the speed of the car drop well below the posted twenty-five-mile-an-hour limit. "We'll try the University Drug first. I think we can case it without going inside. It's worth a try, anyway." A car pulled out from the curbing as he spoke and Dexter backed in, placing us almost in a direct line with the drugstore's double-width plate-glass doors. Without getting out of the car, we could see the cigarette counter with a short man in a too-large topcoat leaning up against it talking to another man with a bald head who stood behind the counter.

Dexter grinned. "Plainclothesman."

I took another look. "How can you tell? He looks just like any man to me."

"That's because you're a sweet unsophisticated child. *I* can tell, though. Anyone who's 'hip' can pick one out in a flash. And if you can't tell by *looking* at him, you can tell by his conversation, see? That's your cue to play innocent. For example, if some character comes sidling up to me and says 'Dropped any lately, man?' I say, 'What, man? What you talking about? Dropped what?'—and then leave as quickly as possible."

A long magazine rack and part of the lunch counter was visible from where we sat. The whole back end of the drugstore, however, was not in view so Dexter said he was going to take a quick look inside. A moment later he was back, shaking his head. "Let's try the Pizza House down the street. Better to walk." He opened the car door for me. I don't know whether somebody had taught him, or if it just came naturally, but Dexter had nice manners.

There was almost no one on the street, but several eating places we passed seemed to be packed with people and I thought we might stop. Dexter, however, pronounced them "square." There was, he said, no chance of Jason being there.

The Pizza House was the place that *looked* square. It had a Merry-Olde-England-type front with thatched roof, white exterior walls crisscrossed with dark wood, and small-paned windows that cast a soft, pinkish glow on the sidewalk.

Inside, it was more Italian than Olde English. Red-and-white checkered tablecloths and candles in wine bottles and that sort of thing. With the exception of a light over the cashier's area and the light shining in above the swinging doors to the kitchen, the candles seemed to provide the only light there was. Actually, it took a little while before I could get my eyes focused well enough to see what was going on. And there wasn't much—considering that practically every table was filled. Over everything was the heavy, sweet smell of pot that I now recognized at the very first whiff.

Dexter nodded to the cashier—a man with longish hair and a little pointed Shakespeare-type beard who immediately went back to reading his magazine—and peered into the dim, smoky recesses of the room. "Well, I guess we'd better find a table and sit down." He sounded rather cross.

We found a small table toward the back of the room and sat so we were facing into it. "At least, he can see us here and if he does, he'll come over." He picked up a menu which was about the size of a newspaper, looked at it and put it back down. "Order something, if you like. But you don't have to. The management doesn't seem to mind one way or the other, now that the place is open again. The police had it closed nearly all of last month."

I ordered a small sausage pizza which I really love but when it came I could only eat about a fourth of it. Dexter kept putting sugar into a cup of coffee which he didn't drink, and watching the front door. Actually, nobody seemed to be eating much. Some small groups apparently were carrying on earth-shattering conversations. Others simply stared into the candles, saying nothing, ignorant even of the presence of their companions. Yet even with the apparent inactivity, people were shuffling about steadily and unobtrusively. The whole thing made me uneasy, particularly what Dexter had said about the police. I was about to suggest that he take me home when his hand closed over mine. "He's here. Just coming in."

I'd expected Jason de Pleine to look a little odd—but not as odd as the man with the red beard making his way across the room toward us. His hair came down in a Mephistophelean peak on his forehead and over his shoulders he wore a long black opera cape of the kind that I'd never seen before except in pictures.

At closer range his beard and hair appeared none too clean, his complexion was pasty and the opera cape had a number of spots.

Dexter leaped up to hold back a chair, tipped his head in my direction. "This is Carla. She knows all about you."

"I hope she doesn't know quite everything, dear boy." He had a cultivated, rather actorish kind of voice.

Dexter, ignoring the reply, leaned forward. "You brought it—the crystals, I mean?"

Jason looked around him, although no one that I could see was paying any attention. "My, er . . . chemist was out of town . . . went east for, you might say, raw materials. However . . ." Jason didn't laugh aloud but his shoulders quivered with mirth beneath his opera cape. I didn't have any idea what he found so funny and, apparently, neither did Dexter. His hand shot out, seizing Jason's bony wrist. "Listen, you———." For the first time I heard Dexter swear. "You promised me if I helped you out you'd supply me. Now you . . . you . . ." Dexter's voice was shaking.

"Dear boy, if you'd let me finish." Jason delicately removed Dexter's hand from his wrist. "If you'd let me finish I would be able to tell you that your virtue is not going to go unrewarded." With two fingers he explored a pocket somewhere under his cape and took out a small, folded piece of paper and pushed it across the table. "A prescription for your grandmother's medicine. Her heart, you know." Again, he quaked silently with laughter.

"You'll have no trouble getting it filled at the University Drug. Everything's in order. It is written on the prescription pad of one of our fair city's most reputable physicians, which I was fortunate enough to, er, pick up. . . ."

He rose, put a hand on Dexter's shoulder. "Oh, one more thing. Be sure and tell your, er, grandmother that dextroamphetamine sulfate is quite powerful medicine and to, er, use it with discretion."

I waited in the car with the motor running while Dexter went in the drugstore. In less than five minutes he was out again. "Just like Jason said. No trouble at all."

I didn't know how he could be so cool. My palms were sweating inside my gloves and my heart was knocking. I knew a stick would make me feel better but I didn't ask for one until we'd gone a dozen blocks or more.

"In my pocket. The right-hand side," Dexter said. "Help yourself."

I fumbled one of the machine-made cigarettes out of a packet that had once held Camels, lighted it from the gadget on the dash and offered it to Dex. "Thanks, no. You can keep the pack." He was smiling. "I'm going to save myself for my Dexies. Do you suppose they're named for me—or me for them? Dexedrine makes pot smoking seem like burning cornsilk."

I put the stick Dexter had refused to my lips and inhaled deeply and let out a little quivering sigh. Soon my uneasiness would go away. I'd feel better soon. I put my head back against the seat. "But you will still be careful," I said. "Jason said to use it with discretion. Remember?"

Dexter laughed. "You don't think I'm crazy, do you? Do you think for a minute that I don't know how to manage? That I don't know how to cool it—and keep it cooled? This isn't my first experience, you know, with something more potent than grass."

I didn't know—and yet I should have. Dexter was always talking about drugs. What this one did, or that one. He studied them. I looked at the burning eye of the stick in my hand and thought about how smart Dexter was. Really smart.

I, myself, felt heavenly. Even inside the car, I seemed to be floating.

"You can manage," I said softly. "If anyone can."

8

ROAD TO NOWHERE

When I came down to breakfast the next morning my mother asked me if I'd had a good time at the party.

"Oh, yes, wonderful!"

I'd never been high at home so early in the day and I liked it. Right after I'd got up, I'd gone in the bathroom, locked the door, turned on the shower, and smoked one of the "machine-mades" that Dexter had given me the night before. I flushed the "roach" down the toilet—such an ugly word, but it really did describe the little screwed-up butt—and squirted some "4711" toilet water around to cover up the smell of burning grass.

"I'm so glad you had a good time," my mother said. "Young people should. It's their *right*."

"Of course, it is," I said. I was at my most agreeable. The truth was, that I liked my mother better when I'd been smoking pot. In any case, I felt sorry for her because I knew she had a hangover. As far as I knew, my mother hadn't had a drink since the day the letter came from Diane saying she was married. And if she had to drink now and then, the night before had been a pretty good time to do it. I knew she hadn't heard me come home.

"I'm going to clean this house today," my mother said virtuously.

I smiled to myself. My mother's words fit the pattern.

She always cleaned the house as penance after she'd been drinking.

"I'm going to clean the house and then I'm going to make a rhubarb pie for your father. I got some rhubarb at the store yesterday that must have been hot-house grown, but it is beautiful. Your father told me last night he's sure to be home in time for dinner." She got up from the table but before she could carry the dishes to the sink she began to cry. "Maybe we'll hear from Diane today."

To make my mother feel better, I said I thought we'd hear from Diane, too, although I really didn't think so. To spare myself an analysis of the situation, I prepared to leave. "If you don't have anything special for me to do, I think I'll study." I really did need to study and it seemed like a good idea to get at it while I was still feeling so high and I seemed to be thinking things through so clearly.

My mother dried her eyes. "I'll be all right. You run along."

Upstairs, I shut the door to my room, then wedged the chair that belongs to my desk under the door knob. I didn't want to be disturbed. Not because I was planning to smoke another joint but because I wanted to think about what had happened after we got back to Lisl's party. After that, I would study.

I straightened the covers on my bed and lay down on it crosswise. I remembered everything that happened, yet it was all sort of fuzzy around the edges. When I shut my eyes little splinters of colored light floated around against the lining of my lids. I thought about the pills that Dexter had got from the druggist on the fake prescription. Mentally, I paused to correct myself. It wasn't a *fake* prescription. Dexter had got exactly what had been called for on the prescription Jason had given him. Doctors prescribed it for . . . for . . . my mind wandered off . . . for whatever it was that they prescribed it for.

Dexter's hand had been steady as he mashed three heart-shaped pink pills into a powder, then poured it carefully into a silver jigger he'd found behind the bar. I watched as he dripped water into the jigger, and muddled the contents with his finger.

I laughed. "Wouldn't it have been simpler just to swallow them whole?"

"Simpler. But I think this is faster." He was really quite serious. "If you're lucky enough to get meth crystals—that's what I thought I was getting from Jason—you can mix it with peanut butter and eat it on bread."

I said, "Oh, yummy! A dextro-amphetamine sulphate sandwich." I laughed—I was, by then, on my second stick—but Dexter was dead serious. "I'm going to drop it now. After that, I don't know how long it will take. I've never had this particular brand before."

This struck me even funnier than the sandwich. "If you drop it right after you've gone to all the trouble of getting it, you're crazy. If you don't want to take it yet, let *me* hold it. I promise not to drop it."

Dexter shook his head, with a patient expression. "You don't know what I'm talking about. 'Drop it' is just an expression. It means you take the drug or whatever, orally. Swallow it—if you still don't dig me. 'Dropping it,' as opposed to 'shooting it up.' That's when you inject it directly into the vein. That's what I'd do now if I'd remembered to bring my equipment."

I shuddered, but Dex only laughed. "I'm going to have to make you a list of words and their meanings so you'll know what I'm talking about."

"It seems to me it would be a lot simpler if you'd just talk English." I'd meant to sound sulky but the words had come out with a giggle.

This time Dex just ignored me. He gave the mixture in the glass another stir then lifted it to his mouth, swallowing it all at once with a rather terrible grimace.

"I can tell by looking at you that it was absolutely scrumpdumptious."

"You're not funny," Dexter said. He wasn't mad, though. He walked around whistling and interrupting conversations that were going on in different parts of the room. Actually, that was all anybody was doing—talking. But the conversation was all very spirited and animated and sounded interesting, particularly that of the two tall, thin brothers who were telling all the reasons they weren't going to register for the draft because they were conscientious objectors. One was going to Canada. But Dexter would have none of any of it, although I'd heard him say lots of times that *he* was going to register for the draft just so he could burn his draft card. He pulled Lisl, who was sitting between the brothers, to her feet. "Let's have some action. Put on some records. If I'd known this party was going to be so dead, Carla and I would never have come back. Hey! I've got an idea. We'll play 'keep away.'" He grabbed a cushion from the couch and hurled it halfway down the room to Chip who leaped up to catch it. The girls screamed and ran around but the boys managed always to keep it out of our reach. Pretty soon, this became tiresome and Lisl, Daisey, Doris, Betty, and I went off by ourselves. As time passed, all the boys but Dexter joined us and we took turns describing how smoking pot made us feel. This was interesting, too, and I think I might even have forgotten Dex was there if Stomper hadn't come over and sat down beside me.

"What's he high on?" He nodded his head toward Dex who was at the far end of the room playing darts by himself. "He's had something stronger than pot. I'd like to know what it was and where he got it. Do *you* know?"

"I know," I said, "but I can't pronounce it. In fact, right at the moment, I can't even remember what it's called." If I could have remembered, I would have told Stomper the name of the drug because in spite of his terrible nickname, I liked him and I know Dex does. They've been friends since they were in kindergarten.

Stomper looked thoughtful. "I hope it isn't meth. But then I guess he'd be too smart to fall for that."

"Don't worry," I said. "Dex can take care of himself." I offered to share the joint I was smoking with Stomper but he shook his head. "Enough's enough. I'm going home. I'll take you, if you want a ride."

"Dex can take me after awhile." Already I was getting tired of talking to Stomper and wished he'd go away. Ideas kept going off in my mind like firecrackers and I wanted to think about them. Stomper's face faded out of my line of vision, then swam back in again. His voice, which had become unintelligible suddenly went off with a bang in my ear. Then he was looking at me very closely—so closely that his eyes both rounded into one huge single one in the middle of his forehead.

Dexter appeared from nowhere. "Where are you going with my girl?"

"Taking her home, fellah."

"Oh, no you're not." Dexter swung at Stomper and missed. He laughed. "What the heck. Take her home. For that matter, take *me* home. This party's dead anyway."

"It's not dead," Stomper said. "It's just over."

I looked around. Daisey Benson and the two tall, thin boys had left. Doris Denman, Betty Baxter, and Chip were milling around with Lisl emptying ash trays. I offered to turn off lights but Lisl said not to; her parents always left a light burning in the house when they went out of town.

I didn't remember much after that except that the ride home had been fun. I'd liked sitting in the car between two boys.

I got up from my bed, walked over to the window, and

97

beginning to wear off. The cure for that was another one. The more I remembered of the events of the night before the more unhappy I became.

I waited until I heard my mother leave in the car for her usual Saturday morning trip to the store, then I took a stick out of the packet that Dexter had given me the night before and went down the hall to the bathroom and locked the door.

Monday morning when I went to school I found a note from Dexter that he'd slipped into my locker. "I think it would be better if we didn't see each other for a while. Explain later." Instead of signing his name, he'd drawn a druggist's prescription symbol: an R with a slanting line drawn through it.

I didn't mind not seeing Dexter. In fact, I was glad for a chance to kind of get caught up with my life. Lately, I'd hardly seen Glenna at all and I was sure her feelings were hurt. Also, this was the week my father was working in Cedar City. So as weeks went, it should be a pretty good one. But it didn't work out that way.

A paper that I'd written for English, one I'd counted on to compensate for a good deal of spotty daily work, came back with a C—and a note written in Mrs. Teeter's flowing penmanship "to come in and see her" after school.

I went, knowing just exactly what she'd say. That she couldn't understand what had happened; that if my work didn't improve I wouldn't make the National Honor Society. I thought she was going to cry and I probably would have cried myself if I hadn't fortified myself with a half a stick in one of the toilets in the girls' rest room before going to see her. I put on a good act and made all kinds of promises but in spite of being a little high the interview made me unhappy.

I told myself I wouldn't smoke any more all that week, but I did. Both at home and at school.

When I did eat lunch, I ate with Doris Denman. Her mother and father had just gotten a divorce but they still kept seeing each other and quarreling. Pot, Doris said, was all that made her life worth living. So we at least had that in common. Glenna and I had less and less. When I'd started hanging around with Dexter at noon, she'd found some other kids to eat lunch with. Sometimes we walked from one class to another together but our conversation was strained and stupid, consisting as it did of Glenna always asking what was wrong with me and with me replying "nothing."

Several times I'd offered to drive her home after school but she'd refused, saying she had a ride. On Thursday, I asked her again and when she said yes, I was happy. I thought that if I tried very hard we could patch things up.

When school was out, she came with me to my locker. The minute I opened it, I saw the note. I snatched it up without reading it and shoved it in a book hoping that Glenna had not noticed. But, of course, she had.

"Aren't you going to read it? It looks like a boy's writing."

"It will keep." I scrabbled around in my locker hoping that Glenna would let the matter drop but she didn't. "I must say you're awfully cool about it. I've seen the day when you would have been leaping for joy if a boy had left a note in your locker."

"If you're going to make a production out of it, I'll read it," I said. "Aloud, if it will make you happy. Perhaps I could buy a spot on KWCC-TV and read it over the air."

"Forget it," Glenna said, shakily. "I . . . I'm sorry I asked."

"I'm going to read it whether you want me to or not," I said angrily. I began fumbling through my books for the note, knowing I was being a beast but unable to help myself. Even the sight of Glenna irritated me—standing there with her big pile of books which she was going to take home and so joyously study in the bosom of her big wonderful family.

However, the minute that I scanned Dexter's note I began to laugh. It wasn't about anything important, at all. "Here," I said. "Read it for yourself. It's only an announcement of a stupid poetry reading." I turned around to hand Glenna the note, but she was already walking swiftly down the hall. I started after her yelling that I was sorry and to wait a minute but she kept right on walking.

When I got home, I read the note again. This is what it said: "Poetry reading tonight at the Old Curiosity Book Store at 8 p.m. Roberto Pinero and others will read from the works of Allen Ginsberg. A discussion period on Ginsberg and Timothy Leary will follow. Orders taken. Everyone welcome."

When I had read it before, it hadn't made sense. Now it did. Dex, with his "cops and robbers" syndrome —syndrome, incidentally, was one of his favorite words —liked to make everything obscure. It would have been simpler, I thought, if he'd simply said that he wanted me to be there.

I didn't have any trouble getting out that night. I simply told my parents that Dexter couldn't take me to a poetry reading at the university because his car was in the garage, but that he'd meet me there.

My parents accepted it all, and of course it was true—except the part about Dexter's car being in the garage. And for all I knew, maybe it was. Anyway, they were glad to have me going someplace as they were having the Newquists over for bridge and "Diane was never home on a weekend night."

When I went out to get my car, my father walked with me and cautioned me about keeping the doors locked while I was driving. He told me that while he was in Los Angeles the past week a bunch of teenagers under the influence of drugs had been arrested while rampaging about the streets and that he was afraid such groups might have infiltrated Cedar City. He said he didn't know what some young people were coming to.

I kissed his cheek and smiled in the darkness. How *quaint* he was! And how surprised he'd be if he could only hear the serious discussions those of us who'd learned "to manage" really had about important things.

It took me so long to find a place to park that by the time I arrived, the poetry reading had started. The place wasn't too big to begin with—a long narrow room lined with bookshelves with an improvised platform at the far end—and it was full. Not only were the closely grouped chairs all occupied but people were standing two or three deep at the back. Standing on the platform and almost obscured by smoke—most of it was from cigarettes or pipes but mingled with it was the unmistakable smell of pot—was a wild-haired, bushybearded man reciting some incomprehensible nonsense in a mournful voice.

I squeezed in between two college students and looked around for Dex. I saw him almost right away and he, I think, had seen me come in. He raised his right hand unobtrusively, and with the palm toward his face shaped his first and second fingers into a V. I grinned. Some time before Dexter had explained to me how the pot-smoker's sign of greeting differed from Winston Churchill's "victory sign": that V was made with the palm facing outward. Not as if one were smoking a cigarette.

Although college kids made up most of the audience —if not college kids they, at least, looked older—I recognized a half dozen or so kids from school.

A few minutes later a new reader went up to the front of the room to take the place of the bearded one and in the general shuffle, Dexter moved into position behind me. He was still so studiedly indifferent that I, too, looked straight ahead listening uneasily to a poem that seemed to consist mostly of a string of dirty words. Several people coughed. A boy and a girl made their way toward the door. During the activity, which was followed by a general turning of heads to see who was leaving, Dexter's hand touched mine, then moved into my coat pocket and was withdrawn. The whole operation was accomplished so unobtrusively that I could have imagined it. But I hadn't—though I didn't know what the small box my exploring fingers found contained until after I got home. That was not long after. For a few minutes later Dexter left, and within another few minutes I left, too. When I reached the street, however, he was nowhere in sight.

My parents were surprised to see me home early. I said I hadn't like the poetry—which was true—and that I thought I'd better spend my time studying. Which was also true.

Mr. and Mrs. Newquist went right on bidding a small slam in spades and I went upstairs, putting the chair in front of my bedroom door. The box I took from my pocket bore the name of the best jewelry store in Cedar City, but that had no significance. There was no reason for Dexter to give me a present, and even if he were giving me one why would he have done it with such secrecy? Still, it was with more curiosity than anything else that I opened the box. Inside, was a plastic sandwich bag filled with about a half cup of something that looked like table salt, and a note asking me to deliver the box to the cashier of the Flower Shoppe—at such and such an address—at two o'clock the next afternoon. Except for an injunction to destroy the note and the promise to explain everything later, that was all.

I unfastened the metal tie that fastened the sack and took a tiny pinch of the saltlike crystals between my fiingers. The stuff had no smell and I couldn't bring myself to taste it. Dex was always telling me about some new and wonderful mind-expanding drug he wanted to try. Perhaps this was one of them. Perhaps the cashier at the Flower Shoppe would give it to Jason's chemist friend to analyze. But whatever was in the sack, didn't matter. Dexter, who had done so much for me, had asked me to do a favor for him. That meant I was going to do it. I tore the note in pieces, flushed them down the john and put the box in my school purse. Too churned up to study, I got ready for bed. It was more important, I decided, to figure out how I was going to get excused from school the next afternoon to keep that two-o'clock appointment.

The lie came easily enough. The next morning I told my mother I had to go to the dentist that afternoon at two o'clock. I said I'd forgotten to tell her that when I'd been the time before—I'm in the last stages of having my teeth straightened—Dr. Carson had had to change my usual after-school appointment to two o'clock because shortly after he was going out of town. "I'll have to have an excuse," I said, "so you may as well write it now."

My mother went to her desk and I stood and looked over her shoulder. I couldn't help smiling. My "excuse" followed the same formula she'd been using since I'd started to kindergarten. I brushed a kiss across her cheek by way of thanks and went back to the kitchen where my father was eating breakfast. I kissed him, too.

"By the way," he said, "let's see those teeth."

I made like a toothpaste ad and he said, "I must say

they've cost me plenty. When I was a kid, I'd never even heard of orthodontia."

My mother said, "Oh, Carl!" to him, and to me, "Daddy's only kidding."

"I know," I said. "Now I've got to rush or I'll be late."

It wasn't really late, but I couldn't wait to get outside. Sometimes the atmosphere of our house was so stifling, the conversation between my mother and father so dull that I thought I would scream. Dexter kept telling me I shouldn't let it get me down.

"If you want to be 'hip,' put up with it passively," he told me. "Use your private time in search of experience that will make you inwardly superior."

The trouble was, I thought, that the only time I felt inwardly superior—and hardly ever outwardly—was when I was smoking pot. This morning I was not feeling superior in any way at all.

9

NO EXIT

I don't know how I could have been so stupid as to think that the Flower Shoppe sold flowers.

Although the address was the same as the one Dexter had given me and there were huge flowers with faces and writhing tortured stems painted on the windows, I walked past the place twice before I caught on. I was still thinking of flowers.

I peered between a couple of giant petals into the interior of the shop. I couldn't see much. Uncovered wooden floors, some psychedelic posters hanging from the walls and ceiling and hand-painted scarves strung from a sort of clothesline at one end of the room.

"It would be best, miss, if you'd move on. The Flower Shoppe's no place for a young girl to hang around."

I turned, guiltily.

The policeman who had addressed me, stood less than two feet away. He was scowling.

I swallowed, licked my dry lips. Somewhere down the street, a clock was striking two. "A scarf . . . I . . . I was just looking at the scarves. I wanted to get one for my . . . kid sister. A present."

"O.K. Go in and buy it, then run along home or back to school or wherever it is that you belong."

I was through the door before he'd finished speaking.

At first glance, the man with the Shakespeare-type beard behind the cash register looked familiar. I'd seen him somewhere before. But not until I'd quaked my way across the room did I remember. This was the same man who'd been in the cashier's cage at the Pizza House the night I went there with Dexter to look for Jason de Pleine.

"You have something for me, yes?" The man's voice was very soft; his lips, against the darkness of his beard, were full and red as blood blisters.

I nodded—afraid, even, to look over my shoulder—then stammered out my story about the policeman who had warned me against coming inside, and the scarf that I now had to buy for my "sister."

"Peace, child." The man with the beard smiled faintly. "Alarm will only give you away. First we will choose a pretty scarf for your, er, sister. Then, while I put it in a sack you can give me the little package and I give you the envelope." Again, the faint smile. "The stupid fuzz sees nothing. He has his back to the door."

I looked at the scarves. Fingering, but not seeing them, I was aware only of the uniformed blue blur outside the window. Finally, I took the scarf nearest me and moved back to where the bearded man waited. Less than a minute later, the little box of white crystals had vanished beneath the counter, an envelope "for my young man" disappeared into my purse and a sack containing a scarf for which I did not pay was placed in my hand.

The policeman stepped to one side as I opened the door. I held out the sack so he could see I'd made a purchase, then forced myself to walk—not run—until I reached my car.

By the time I got back to school I was feeling all right. I still had ten minutes to spare before the bell rang for my next class.

In the girls' rest room, I nodded to my image in the long mirror above the bank of lavatories. I couldn't help feeling rather pleased with the way things had gone. And how easily that policeman had been taken in! Almost anything could have been in the box I'd delivered and he would never have known. Dexter would laugh when I told him. It was all part of the "cops and robbers" game he liked playing. Dexter would laugh at the scarf, too. Printed in supposedly psychedelic hues and patterns, it really was hideous. Dexter was hip, but he wasn't a hippie. There was a difference.

I stuffed the scarf in my purse and took out the envelope the man had given me. I'd almost forgotten that I had it.

It was not addressed and when I turned it over I could see that although it had been sealed the flap, in places, was beginning to pull away. A second later, it had given completely beneath my prying finger.

I don't know what I had expected to find—and now I know it was pretty stupid of me not to have guessed—but not what I did. Money. Even then, I had the packet of bills in my hand before I noticed that they were *hundreds*. My fingers shook as I counted them. *Fifteen* hundreds. Fifteen hundreds was one thousand, five hundred dollars. A little drift of darkness, like smoke, passed in front of my eyes. I leaned forward, bracing myself against the cold white lavatory until it passed. A moment later the bell rang, giving me but a moment to stuff the envelope and money into my purse before the stampede into the rest room began. Then I went to find Dex.

I didn't much count on running into Dex and I didn't. But not until school was out did I discover that he was absent. Mr. Dieter, Dex's home-room teacher, told me he'd been absent two other days that week, also. He then went on to ask a lot of personal, prying questions that I resented. Like did I know if anything was "troubling" Dexter, just how well I was acquainted with him, and had I ever met his parents. He said that Dex was an uncommonly bright boy with unusual promise and that he'd like to help him if he could.

I answered that I knew Dexter hardly at all—though I don't think he believed me—so I was hardly the person to tell if anything was troubling him, and got out of there as fast as I could. What was troubling *me* was the money I was carrying around.

I'd changed its hiding place twice since I'd got home from school. I wanted it out of the house. And I wanted an explanation from Dexter. I knew there'd be one. He always had reasons, good reasons, for everything he did. But I wanted to hear them just the same.

Later that evening when my parents said they were going out, I was glad. I could be as nervous as I pleased without any questions being asked. I milled around the house, tried to study and gave it up, watched some stupid program on TV for a little while and then decided if Dex wasn't going to call me I'd call him.

I let the phone ring about forty times before I remembered that Dex had told me his grandmother was going to be out of town. Something to do with a poverty program for the Seminole Indians. Whenever Mrs. Smith was away, her housekeeper went to visit her daughter, leaving Dex to "batch it."

A knock came at the front door just as I hung up. I'm not afraid when I'm home alone, still I always turn on the light and look out to see who it is before opening up. It was Dex. He signaled for me to turn off the porch light and I did before opening the door.

The minute he was inside, my nervousness gave way to

irritation. "Now that you're here," I said, "maybe you can tell me what was in that package I delivered to the Flower Shoppe that was worth fifteen hundred dollars. Maybe I can find out where you've been. Today, when I went looking for you Mr. Dieter asked all kinds of questions. You're not sick, are you?" The truth was, I thought, that Dexter did look sick. He was perspiring heavily, something I'd never seen him do before, and his hand shook as he offered me a stick from the Camel package. I grabbed it. People who try to make a case for pot may tell you it isn't addictive. If by that they mean you don't go crazy if you can't get it, I suppose they're right. But you can still want it to the point where you're about ready to jump out of your skin.

I lighted the stick, inhaled, and held the smoke in my lungs as Dex prowled around the living room, circling twice before he answered me.

"Sick? Of course, I'm not sick. I may have lost a little weight because I've had more important things on my mind than stuffing myself with a lot of food." He stopped in front of me. His eyes were brilliant, the big black pupils almost engulfing the blue. "I've been experimenting. Finding *answers*. Thinking . . . making plans . . . I've been working on a book. . . ."

A shiver trickled down my spine. I couldn't help it when Dex talked like that. I remembered what Mr. Dieter said about Dex having unusual promise.

"It's good, Car, really good. It . . . it's important." He'd started circling again. I'd seen wild animals in cages at the zoo pacing restlessly, relentlessly, in the same way. I stood in front of him to make him stop. "I want to hear about your book. I want to read it, if you'll let me. But first, tell me what was in that box. I . . . I've got to know. Did I do anything wrong? Anything against the law?" Even the pot

I'd smoked couldn't keep me from trembling.

"Listen, Car." Dex gripped me by my elbows so fiercely that I winced. "I'm going to tell you the truth. Meth crystals were in that box, and selling it *is* against the law. But it's not wrong, see? There's a difference. Anything that makes you feel so beautiful, *can't* be wrong." He was becoming excited again. "The law says that selling marijuana is wrong. Even having it in your possession is a crime. If the narcs caught me giving you that stick you just smoked, they could put me in jail. Yet, your mother and my father and about a million other people can get stinking drunk anytime they want to. Whiskey, gin, wine. You name it. They can buy it by the carload. But if it's a drug . . . if it's marijuana or meth or LSD or a barb or a yellow jacket or a redbird—any drug that helps you open your eyes wide so you can really *see* things and helps you learn to understand yourself, they're against it. That's why we have to help each other. If Jason had gone anywhere near the Flower Shoppe today with that packet of meth, the narcs would have got him. They've got their eye out for me, too, though they haven't anything to go on. That's why I asked you to make the drop. Jason's lying low for a while. The chemist is going to route everything through me, and maybe it will just go on that way. Jason wasn't really as smart as he should have been. That queer get-up just attracted attention. It had got so that the minute he stepped foot into the Pizza House or the Flower Shoppe or the University Drug, the fuzz knew something would be changing hands."

"I thought you liked him." I really wasn't understanding all Dex said.

"I did like him. I do. But all things must change to something new and something strange. I don't know who said that, but it expresses what I think—what I believe."

Dexter paused, stared at nothing, then started for the door. "Let's go."

"Go where?"

"A . . . a place. A place I've fixed up."

"I can go. I guess." I spoke slowly, not sure I even wanted to go at all.

Dex scowled. "What do you mean you 'guess' you can go? There's nobody around to stop you."

Dex was right, of course. There wasn't anybody to stop me. If Dex left I'd be alone with myself and I didn't find myself very good company any more.

"O.K.," I said, "I'll go."

I scribbled a note to my parents, then went upstairs to get the money from its hiding place. Before I could get back down, the phone rang. "I'll get that," I yelled, but I was too late.

Dex, wearing a cat-and-canary smile, had just hung up

"That was for me, wasn't it?"

Dex grinned.

"It was a boy, too."

"Of course. If it had been a girl, I would have called you."

A little sob caught in my throat as Dexter reached for me, but I pulled away. Again, he caught up with me, put his arms around me, and held me so close that I could feel his eyelashes brush against my cheek. "If you're sore, I'm sorry. But it wouldn't work—you and that fellow whoever he was. Just that little while I talked to him, I could tell he was square. You need someone like me—and I need someone like you."

In all the times we'd been together, it was the nicest thing he'd ever said to me. Dex was real. And dreaming about Tom Willard was . . . well, dreaming. Tom *was* square. And I was—crooked. The time we might have been friends was over the hill and long ago. I managed a smile and took the hand that Dex held out to me.

"It's just such a perfect place I don't know why I never thought of it before," Dex said. "Listen. You can hear the lapping of the water." I listened and I could hear it. The lapping. It was mixed in with all the other nighttime noises that really aren't noises at all but the smallest and almost inaudible of sounds. The rustle of leaves one against another as the wind moved through them, a twig snapping, a small bird's cry, a kind of gentle sigh that was my own breathing.

We'd left the car on the road, and although Dexter said it wasn't far to the shack it seemed as if we'd been walking quite a while. An almost full moon was rising between the branches of the trees and although it did not shed enough light for me to see the path, when Dexter said, "There's the shack, in the clearing just ahead," I could see its outlines.

"My father used to like to come out here with some of his pals and they'd sit around and fish and get drunk together. But Mae, that's the wife my father has now, didn't like the idea of him coming out here and goofing around any better than my own mother did. So he doesn't come any more. Someday, he'll sell it and make a lot of money. I guess he's holding it for that. Property this close to the city and right on the river is getting scarce. But until he sells it, I'm using it. If my father knew, he wouldn't care. I've even been coming out here at night since I've had the electricity turned on." He laughed. "Water I can do without." Pausing, he felt before him with his foot and said, "It's kind of squishy here. You'd better jump."

I jumped, fell against him so hard I almost knocked him over. We rocked with helpless laughter. We both were pretty high.

Dexter unlocked the padlock on the door of the shack with a key he took from his pocket—he said he'd wrecked the old padlock the first time he'd broken in—and turned on a light just inside the door.

I think if Dexter hadn't gone on and on about how great he'd fixed everything up, I might not have expected quite so much. But considering that he'd spent the greater part of the three days he'd been absent from school that week out there, I thought it looked crummy. He'd nailed some pieces of dark material over the windows and thrown a grubby white chenille spread over a mattress on the floor. The two built-in bunks had neither mattresses nor bedding. The only decent thing in the place was a brand-new portable typewriter that sat in the middle of the floor. Beside it was a pile of manila paper, a file folder that Dex said held the book he was working on, and an overflowing ash tray.

There wasn't much in the kitchen, either, but Dex was bursting with excitement as he threw open the door of a beat-up-looking refrigerator. "Look, Car, this is what I really wanted you to see."

I stared, first bewildered and then aghast. There was enough stuff on the shelves to stock a drugstore. There were small bottles of pills and colored capsules, bigger bottles of cough syrup. There were nasal inhalers, asthma remedies, and tranquilizers. On one shelf there must have been a dozen tubes of glue.

"Where . . . where did it all come from?"

Dexter's eyes were brilliant. "I'd tell you, Car, but it's best if you don't know. If the narcs found this stuff, I'd be out of luck. It . . . it's my private stock. Each drug, each thing—even the glue—does something special. Does its . . . certain thing. I'm analyzing them, studying them, being really scientific." He took out a half dozen small bottles as he talked, lined them up on the counter. "These pink 'crossroads,' the pale green ones, and the peach-colored ones are amphetamines. The orange hearts are dextroamphetamine sulphates—like the ones Jason gave me that first prescription for—so are these 'footballs' and the green triangles. All of these take you up. Turn you on. And these"—he lined up another row of bottles as he talked—"bring you down."

From far away, I could hear Dexter calling out a litany of their names. "Yellow jackets," "blue heavens," "redbirds" . . . "barbs." The humming of the refrigerator was suddenly roaring like a jet engine in my ears. Something was happening that I didn't like at all. The floor of the shack swam up to meet me, then receded. I tried to remember how many sticks I'd smoked that night. Two, I remembered. Three? Or had it been even more. I remembered the time I'd offered to share a stick with Stomper and he said he'd had enough. Maybe, I'd had enough. Maybe too much. Maybe pot, in spite of what people said, could hurt you after all. I put my hands up under my bangs. They were damp with perspiration.

I called out Dexter's name in the high tinny voice I used to use when I "talked" for my doll when I was a little girl. I'd always "talked" for Diane's doll, too, because I was better at thinking of things for them to say. I didn't know I was crying, until I felt a tear splash on my arm. *I wanted to see Diane. Crazy as it was, I wanted to see my mother. I wanted to go home.*

From a jar of water on the counter, Dexter dribbled a few drops into the spoon that held the powder, wiggled it gently, then drew the solution up through a tiny piece of cotton into a plastic eyedropper.

I looked away, then back again. A short, red needle had been twisted into the dropper. Dex was smiling, almost beautiful. He made a fist of his left hand and brought the point of the needle down toward the fine blue vein on his bare arm. "I'm going to shoot it now." His voice was soft, almost tender.

"No! Dexter, don't! Dexter, please!"

My words were lost in a single piercing scream. Whether it was my own, or Dexter's, I never knew.

10

ME, MYSELF, AND I

The eyedropper with the needle still in it was dangling from Dex's arm when I found him. How long he'd lain sprawled outside the shack, or how long my own blackout lasted, I had no way of knowing.

Shutting my eyes, I pulled the needle from the vein, then pressed my fingers over the place on his wrist where the pulse should be. Minutes passed before I found it, and even then it was so faint and so erratic that it was almost stifled by the beating of my own heart.

All I remembered about first aid, learned summers ago at camp, was that if any bones were broken I should not try to move him. And I could not have moved him if I tried. Even his head, when I tried to put my folded sweater beneath it so it would not rest against a stone, was heavy. In the rectangle of light that shone from the shack's open door, I looked at my hands and knew that the dark, sticky substance on them was blood.

I needed help, yet as far as we were from the road, I could have screamed until my voice was gone and no one would hear me. And if help came, if the police came, what then? I thought of all the stuff Dex had in the refrigerator. I remembered Dex saying that if the narcs found it, he'd go to jail for years. *But that must not happen. I wasn't going to let it.*

In the kitchen, I looked for a sack and not finding one

grabbed a rag hanging from a nail near the sink. Once a dish towel, it was big, square, and looked fairly strong. Onto it, I dumped everything in the refrigerator, including a plastic bag of grass I'd not noticed before, and tied the four corners together.

The improvised sack was heavy and unmanageable but I could lift it. And I knew if I could lift it, I could somehow manage to carry it to the car.

Outside, I once again crouched beside Dex. The bloody stain on my sweater had grown larger but he had not moved. And his pulse was still there. I searched his pockets until I found the keys to the car, then I made the sign of the cross. I'm not a Catholic—not anything—but I'd seen Glenna cross herself a thousand times. It didn't seem right to go off and leave Dex, even if that is what I had to do, without asking God to watch over him until help came.

There were so many cars parked outside the first roadside restaurant that I passed, I knew I dared not stop there to use the phone. Taking the unfamiliar path from the shack to the road where we'd left the car, and with the heavy and unyielding bag banging at my knees, I'd fallen a half dozen times. My dress was muddy and my stockings torn. I could only guess how I looked.

I drove on. I passed two brightly lighted filling stations and another roadside eating place before I saw the little diner. Even as I slowed, I could see it was shabby. The red neon sign spelling out "Dewdrop Inn" flickered feebly. There was a "Closed" sign in the window but a phone booth stood nearby. I stopped the car and leaving the motor running, stumbled toward it. Inside, with the heavy phone book dangling from its chain in my hands, I fumbled through the pages until I found Stomper's number.

My dime pinged into the slot. Halfway through the

dialing, I made a mistake and had to start again. The phone rang a dozen times. When a woman's sleepy voice said "hello," it took me a moment to collect myself. Somehow, I'd thought it would be Stomper, himself, who would answer.

"Who is this?" As soon as I had spoken the woman's voice became sharp and no longer sleepy.

"A . . . a friend. Is . . . is Stomper there?"

"Daryl is sleeping." The woman spoke as if this ended it, but she did not go away.

"Please." I tried again. "I really do have to speak to him. A friend of his . . . a boy . . . asked me to call. It's an emergency."

Cars whizzed passed on the highway, but none turned into the "Dewdrop Inn." It seemed forever before Stomper said, "Hello." That single word was spoken so cautiously that not until after I'd finished telling him what had happened and what had to be done, was I certain that he was still listening.

"It's too bad. Terrible," he said at last, "but I don't know what I can do."

"I know what you can do!" I knew I was screaming into the phone, but I couldn't help myself. All the control and calmness I'd exercised in bringing my plan this far to completion had left me with nothing at all. "You can call the police. You can help them find the shack. You can find out if . . . if Dex is still alive."

Stomper swore. It brought me around. "Don't lose your head, you little fool. You're the one who is going to have to call the police. I'm not going to get involved. I've put pot-smoking and all that kid-stuff behind me. It's not my bag any more."

I hung up, called the police, and gave them the best instructions for finding Dex that I could. I felt quite peaceful and no longer afraid. Soon Dex would be on his way to the hospital. Soon all the evidence on the seat beside me would be lying on the bottom of the lagoon in Parula Park where no one—not even Dex—would ever find it. Best of all, I'd be almost home.

I was less than a mile from the entrance to the park when I first became aware of the spinning light behind me. It made no impression. I was thinking of the little path that led down to the lake. How dark the footbridge would be. There would be no one to watch as I uncapped the bottles and dropped the pills and the capsules, the syrups and all the rest into the gentle water. For the ice had been gone for months now. The skaters in their bright jackets and tasseled caps, like figures from a Grandma Moses painting, were all dispersed. Never again would Dexter and I watch them from the top of our private hill. I felt tears slipping down my cheeks. Brushing them away, I pressed my foot on the accelerator and welcomed the rush of air against my face. The spinning light grew closer. A dark car drew abreast of me and pressed me to the curb.

"All right. Let's have your driver's license." A bulky, uniformed figure blocked the open window beside me. "Don't panic. Take your time." It was not a kindly voice, but neither was it a voice of a person who hates kids.

I knew I had my driver's license. It should be in its own little case, but my fingers fumbled uselessly among all the junk that collects at the bottom of a big pouch purse.

"O.K., kid." The voice was patient, resigned. "Dump it all out on the seat and I'll hold my light."

I didn't want to dump it. I didn't want any flashlight shining on the lumpy bundle on the seat beside me. I hadn't even looked at it since I'd put it in the car.

One by one, I started to take things out of my purse and put them in my lap.

"On the seat, sister. Like I said."

With the white circle of light focused on the contents of my purse, I saw my driver's license right away. But that wasn't all. Spilling out on the blue upholstery was a bottle of pink, heart-shaped pills and a sprinkling of coarse, brown tobaccoish crumbs.

"I'm placing you under arrest for speeding. But it is my duty to warn you that you have the right to remain silent." The words, echoing and reverberating, seemed to come from far away. ". . . anything you say . . . used against you in a court of law . . . right to talk to a lawyer . . . have him present while you are being questioned . . ." I closed my eyes. None of this was happening. Not to *me*. It was a bad dream from which I would awaken. I dug my fingernails into the flesh of my crossed arms and felt the sudden pain.

The voice, natural now, was close to my ear. "You do understand what I've been telling you. If not, I'll go through it once again."

"I . . . I understand."

A thumb was jerked. "Into the back seat of the patrol car."

Inside the car, it was as light as on a stage. Outside, the spinner threw circles of revolving light into the shadows. Passing cars slowed and moved on. The officer was speaking into the intercom. "Mulcahey at Fifty-third and Park. Need assistance. Car stopped for speeding. One white, female juvenile. Suspicion of marijuana and narcotic drugs. Car registered in the name of Dexter Smith. . . ."

I lay down on the seat, drew my knees up to my chest, and with one arm tried to shield my eyes from the light. Many times in my life I'd been unhappy, but never before had I wished that I was dead.

I worried about the hearing until I was sick. But everyone was very nice. Two of my teachers, Mr. Reedy and Mrs. Teeter, testified in my behalf. Even the girls advisor, who everyone thinks has ice water in her veins instead of blood, said I should have another chance.

If they hadn't, I'd now be in Eldorville, where the girls' reformatory is, instead of being on probation.

At the hearing, when it came my turn to talk and I told why I had all those pills and other stuff in my possession, I wasn't the only one who cried. The judge had told me to tell the truth, and I did. Everybody in that room knew I couldn't hurt Dex, no matter what I said.

Even after being home sick for a week, what I dreaded most was going back to school. My name hadn't been in the paper—they've got a policy against it if you're not yet eighteen—still everybody in town had read the story about the teen-ager who'd been picked up by police with a car full of drugs. And every kid going to Cedar City High knew it was me. If it hadn't been for Glenna, who never once mentioned what had happened, I don't think I'd have gotten through the week.

About fifty percent of the kids who wanted to talk to me about it, weren't interested in me at all. Dex was the one they wanted to hear about. Was it true, they asked with pious righteousness, that Dex was a "meth monster" now? Had he really "freaked out?" Was a "flower child" a person who had flipped on speed? Would Dex be back to graduate, they wondered, or was he "bombed" for good?

I said I didn't know. It was the truth but they didn't believe me. At the hospital, Dex had apparently been classified top secret and although I called almost every day to ask how he was, the only reply I ever received was that he was resting comfortably.

The other fifty percent of the kids I talked to were what you might call "on my side." Marcie was typical. Her expression was subdued as she waited for me one afternoon after class, but inside she was like a kettle on the verge of boiling over.

"I just wanted to tell you that I think you're brave and wonderful, and that I admire you for what you did for Dex." She looked over her shoulder to see if anyone was listening and although no one was, she dropped her voice. "If he hadn't started messing around with drugs and had just stuck to marijuana he wouldn't be . . . well, like he is. Lisl Camp told me that marijuana isn't habit-forming or anything. I'd try it myself but if my parents found out, they'd murder me. In cold blood."

"Then you'd better not try." For a bright girl, Marcie Hamilton was uncommonly stupid.

Marcie was aghast. "Oh, I wouldn't! It's just that I can't help admiring those people who have the courage to follow their own thing. If a person has thought it through and made, well, a rational decision, I think it's O.K., don't you?"

"No," I said, "I don't." I know I sounded sour, but the truth was that Marcie's talk about "rational decisions" and people doing their "own thing" was almost more than I could stand to listen to. I wondered what she'd say if I told her I had smoked pot, not because of any soul-searching, but that I'd gotten into it by accident. And that once I'd gotten in, I didn't know how to get out. For a while, smoking pot had made me forget how lousy and un-satisfactory my life really was. But nothing had really changed. Now I knew that the only thing that would change it much was me.

My father opened the front door as I came up the steps. He hadn't been out of town since the night he and my mother had been called to the police station. And as soon as I was back in school, he always managed to be home when I got there. In a way, it irritated me. What did he ex-pect me to do, I wondered—come home, puffing away with a stick in each hand? And in another way, it just made me sad. It was as if, by being there to give me a hearty greeting when I came home from school, he was paying some long overdue account.

Now, too, my mother was always lurking around somewhere in the background, and I knew that after I'd gone up to my room—there was nowhere else to go—she and my father went off by themselves and talked me over.

My father put an arm around my shoulder as I came through the door. "How's my girl?" he said. "How was everything today?"

I said, "Oh, about as usual," then realizing that "as usual" wasn't very good, I amended it to "fine." We both were really trying, and that counted for a lot.

My mother emerged from somewhere. "Well," she said gaily, "you certainly hit the jackpot. Two letters. And this one certainly looks as if it had been around." She handed it to me, keeping the other, while I examined it. Mis-addressed in the first place, it had been stamped "No such person at this address" and marked "Return to sender." After that, it had been sent on its way again. Now the various cancellation marks obliterated almost everything except my name.

My mother tilted her head to look at it again. "Have you any idea who it's from?"

I said I didn't, and I knew she was disappointed when I put it in my pocket without opening it. Reluctantly, she gave me the letter she still held. "I don't know who this one could be from, either. The name and address is printed, but even so it looks as if it *could* be from Diane." My mother's chin trembled and she turned away, holding her handkerchief over her mouth.

"Anita! Stop that!" My father spoke in the sharp, imperative tone a parent uses to stop a child from gouging holes in a piece of furniture.

My mother stopped it.

124

When she'd started having hysterics at the police station the night I was arrested, my father had yelled, "For God's sake shut up" at her, and she had.

I took my letters and went up to my room. I opened the one from Diane first. Like my mother, I could tell by looking at it that it was from her.

I read it, cried for a long time, then read it again. The Associated Press had picked up the story about the Cedar City teen-ager who had been arrested with a lot of drugs in her possession, and Diane wondered if I had been involved. Even before that, though, she had been wanting to come home. Twice, she'd had Nick call Long Distance, hoping that I would answer the phone so he could find out how the land lay. That hadn't worked out. The first time my mother answered. (That was the disastrous night that Dex almost ran over me.) After asking to speak to me and finding I wasn't there, Nick had simply hung up. The second time he called, Dex had answered the phone so he had fared no better than before. Now that Nick's unit had been shipped to the South Pacific, Diane was coming home, no matter what her welcome. She felt bad, because she was sure she'd let me down.

The other letter was from Tom. From some place in Utah, so small that it doesn't even show on the map. He said he knew, when he met me, that I'd bring him luck, only he didn't think that things would happen quite so fast. But they had. The day after Marcie's party, the company he'd worked for the summer before called to say that they were recruiting men to build a government airfield in the desert. The pay was good, and he packed up and left two days later. That was almost all, but what he said at the end of the letter after asking me to be sure and write him—made me get up and look at myself in the mirror. I couldn't see what Tom had seen, but it was nice to know that it is there.

125

I took a shower, put a ribbon on my hair, and hunted around until I found some lipstick. Then I went downstairs and told my parents that Diane was coming home.

I don't know why they finally decided I could go see Dex, but they did. Diane drove me over in my car. We didn't talk much on the way, mostly because our jaws had hardly stopped wagging since she got home. She waited in the car and wrote a letter to Nick while I went in. She writes him every day and most days she hears from him. I don't think that I mentioned that Nick isn't an Italian, or a Greek, or Mormon or anything, but just a boy. When he gets out of the army he's going back and finish college. He enlisted because he didn't want the draft hanging over him, Diane says, and she's going back to college herself this fall.

There are huge lawns all around the hospital. Patients who are well enough stroll there or sit and visit with friends who've come to call. A woman at a desk inside directed me to the third floor and a nurse took me down to Dex's room. Except for bedroom slippers he was dressed, and other than being awfully thin he didn't look sick at all. He was seated before a portable typewriter, and for a moment I thought he was smoking. But as I drew nearer, I saw that there was nothing in his hand.

I said, "Hello, Dex."

"Oh, hello there," he said. "Come in. I'm working on my book but you won't disturb me."

"I'm glad you're working," I said. "Do you mind if I look?"

"I'm not really far enough along for you to tell what it's about. But it's going to be good. It . . . it's important."

I stood beside him, looking down at the sheet of paper in the machine. Like the pages in the file folder at the shack that I'd later seen, the few words he'd strung together made no sense at all.

I turned away. "I think it might be better if I waited . . . waited till you're through."

After that, Dex seemed to forget all about me and pretty soon I left.

Dexter's father was waiting outside the door and we talked for a few minutes about how I thought Dex looked and what the doctors said. The trouble was, nobody knew for sure how many drugs Dex had experimented with or in what concentrations, so they couldn't tell for sure what the outcome would be.

I've not seen Dex since, but I've been thinking about him a lot. And me. That's why I called Dex's father and asked him if he cared if I used the shack until he got ready to put it on the market. He said no, to go ahead.

That's where I am now. I know I can't write the book Dex thought he would write. But maybe I can tell a story of a different kind. The best first sentence of the best book I ever read keeps coming back to me. Maybe writing "Call me Carla" would be a good place to begin.